VOICES

Soleiman
Fayyad

VOICES

A Novel

Translated
from the Arabic
with an introduction by

Hosam Aboul-Ela

Marion Boyars
New York · London

First published in the United States and Great Britain in 1993 by
Marion Boyars Publishers
237 East 39th Street, New York, New York 10016
24 Lacy Road, London SW15 1NL

Distributed in Australia by
Peribo Pty Ltd, Terrey Hills, NSW

© Soleiman Fayyad 1986
© English translation Marion Boyars Publishers 1993

Revised edition published in 1977 by Editions Kutub Arabiya, Cairo, under the title *Aswat*

Library of Congress Cataloging-in-Publication Data
Fayyād Sulaymān
　　[Aswāt. English]
　　Voices/Soleiman Fayyad; translated from the Arabic by Hosam
Aboul-Ela.
　　Translation of Aswat
　　I.Title
　　PJ7824.A95A913 1992
　　892'.736-dc20   92-13638

British Library Cataloguing in Publication Data
Fayyad, Soleiman
　　Voices
　　I. Title II. Aboul-Ela, Hosam
　　892.736 [F]

ISBN 0–7145–2945–1 Cloth

Typeset in 11/13 pt Baskerville and Gill Sans light by
Ann Buchan (Typesetters), Shepperton
Printed and bound in Great Britain by
Biddles Ltd, Guildford and King's Lynn

Introduction

B orn in the eastern region of the Nile delta in 1929,
Soleiman Fayyad published his first collection of
short stories in Cairo in 1961, five years after obtaining a
degree from Al-Azhar University in Cairo. Over the
course of his career he has published eight volumes of
short stories and the novel, *Voices*, as well as several
children's books and dictionaries of Arabic grammar and
usage.

Beyond these bare facts, the task of introducing
Fayyad and his work is difficult since both the man and
the work tend to slip between the epochs, themes and
styles which exemplify traditional categorizations of

modern Egyptian literature. Fayyad was born after the two standard bearers of the generation traditionally credited with laying the foundation for contemporary Egyptian narrative — Naguib Mahfouz, the Nobel Prize winning novelist, and Yusuf Idriss, usually considered the father of the modern Egyptian short story. At the same time, he is older than many of the writers associated with Egypt's 'generation of the sixties', a group whose intellectual formation was dramatically influenced by the coming to power of Gamal Abdel Nasser and the country's subsequent two and a half decades of confrontation with Israel and the West. Like many of the younger generation of writers, Fayyad was a student when Nasser led the free officers in a revolt against British interests which eventually led to the abdication and exile of King Farouk in July of 1952. He began writing at the zenith of Nasser's popularity and had become a skilled writer by the time of Nasser's great defeat in 1967.

This means that politics in general, and Western hegemony in particular, were as important a theme for Fayyad as for other writers who developed intellectually in Nasser's Egypt. In fact, in 1969 Fayyad published a volume of short fiction directly in response to the defeat of '67.

But it should be made clear that Fayyad's reputation has grown from less overtly political material. His intense interest in rural Egypt is more characteristic of early writers like Muhammad Hussein Haykal, Tawfik al-Hakim, or Abdel Rahman al-Sharqawi, and his precise depictions of the psychological makeup of his characters rivals some of the finest work of Mahfouz and Idriss.

If then the author could be defined as a writer who slips between the categories, his novel *Voices* is an equally uncategorizable book. First written in 1972 after a brief visit to East Germany, marking the author's first trip outside the Arab world, *Voices* was revised by Fayyad in 1977 and again in 1990 and is his only novel, his most popular and (by any imaginable measure) his best work. It combines all of the themes mentioned above — the East–West confrontation, rural Egypt, and psychological emphasis — to create a work which flies in the face of Arabic literature's conventional wisdoms.

When the police commissioner refers in the final pages of the novel to two other well known Egyptian novels, Yahya Haqqi's *The Saint's Lamp* and Al-Hakim's *Bird from the East*, he is invoking a well-worn novelistic genre which takes the clash between Orient and Occident as its subject matter. Both these novels (and many others like them) tell the story of a young Egyptian male who travels to Europe on a voyage of discovery. These novels inevitably end up asserting through their events the ethical superiority of the East over the technologically advanced but morally decadent West.

Structurally, *Voices* is the exact converse of these novels. Instead of an Arab male travelling to Europe, a French woman comes to Egypt; instead of seeing everything through the eyes of this central figure, we see nothing through her eyes; instead of everything leading to resolution, everything leads only to bitterness. Could it be that after what happened in 1967 the Egyptian intelligentsia found no solace in being morally superior but technologically backward? Or that the whole idea of this moral superiority had become meaningless?

The English reader should not overlook the way the novel reinforces this theme of East–West conflict by deftly working into the background references to virtually every French military venture in Egypt since recorded history began. The first of these references occurs in the penultimate section of the first chapter when the village Omda makes an extended reference to Napoleon's invasion of Egypt. French forces occupied the country from 1798 to 1801, but despite the brevity of the occupation, its impact on Egyptian society was dramatic and long-lasting. Supposedly, Egyptians saw their language printed for the first time when the French troops distributed handbills printed on an Arabic press which Napoleon had brought with him. For this and other reasons, traditionalist critics often argue that the event marked the beginning of a modern literary renaissance in Egypt after 1801. The French who stayed behind after Napoleon's departure and assimilated into Egyptian society, generally did so in the villages in the eastern half of the Nile delta, where *Voices* is set.

The subtext of Franco-Egyptian conflict is thrown even further back at the beginning of the third Section when Simone and Mahmoud Ibn al-Munsi visit the museum and house of Ibn-Luqman in the town of Mansura in the eastern delta region. Here the reference is to the final offensive of the crusades initiated by an attack on Egypt led by the French King Louis IX in the summer of 1249. In the spring of 1250 French forces were defeated; Louis was taken prisoner and jailed in Man-sura. There he was held in the house of the secretary, Fakhr ad-Din Ibn-Luqman and guarded by a Eunuch named Sabih Al-Mu'azzami who, some legends say, castrated the king about whom medieval poet Jamal ad-Din Ibn-Yahya wrote the lines of poetry quoted in that passage. Several weeks later French forces agreed to leave Egypt, and their king was released.

When Simone and the Egyptian student, Mahmoud Ibn al-Munsi, discuss the crusade during the visit, the apparent nonchalance of the Frenchwoman contrasts with the hypersensitivity of the young Egyptian, and at this point (as throughout the novel) psychology and politics meet.

I would be remiss if I didn't thank several friends: Abbas al-Tonsi, Mohamed Aboul-Ela, Jean Aboul-Ela, Ayman El- Desouky, Chris Hudson and Robert Macdonald who provided help of various types. I would also like to thank Marion Boyars Publishers for their encouragement and assistance; and I would particularly like to thank the author for the honor of being associated with this story, which — as the reader is about to see — could hardly be more powerful.

Table of Narrators

THE MAAMUR: police commissioner from the nearest metropolitan area responsible for security and other administrative functions in an area including the village of Darawish.

MAHMOUD IBN AL-MUNSI: advanced high school student, famous throughout the village for his precocious intellect.

AHMED AL-BAHAIRI: village shopkeeper whose life is overturned by the return of his long lost elder brother from France.

THE OMDA: appointed administrative chief of the village, usually chosen from the village's most propertied (and thus most politically powerful) family.

HAMID AL-BAHAIRI: native son of Darawish whose entire adult life has been spent in France.

UM AHMED: mother of Ahmed and Hamid. 'Um' means 'mother of' and is often used in rural areas and among the urban working-class with the name of the first-born son instead of the mother's own name. Because of Hamid's disappearance in childhood she has taken the name of her remaining son.

ZEINAB: wife of Ahmed.

THE RETURN

The Maamur

The time was precisely 10 o'clock. I sat at my desk
and unfastened the top buttons of my shirt to dry
my perspiration and relieve my suffering from the smoth-
ering humidity. The soldier brought me my morning
coffee, and I began to drink it leisurely as I ran my eyes
through my favorite morning paper, then scrutinized the
presiding officer's reports regarding yesterday's inci-
dents. I didn't find anything worthy of my attention: just
the usual petty crimes that happen every day and that I
was more than used to. They barely aroused my curiosity now. I closed the file and leaned my cheek against my
fist — elbow propped against the arm of my chair — and

let my thoughts wander through various and sundry trivialities.

Then the soldier opened the door again, pushed it shut behind him and clicked his heels together. It was not time for the mail yet, but he thrust toward me an envelope that looked, from its shape and the rectangular cellophane window containing my name and official title, like a telegram. I felt a sudden anxiety, expecting some sort of problem, the kind I'm always watching out for whenever I see a telegram. But I feigned composure and waved away the soldier, who promptly left me free to tear the envelope open. I shifted into a state of extreme attention and began to feel as though I were waking suddenly from a long nap. The telegram had been sent from Europe: Paris to be precise. I double checked to be sure that it really was addressed to me and had not come by mistake, then was overcome by an uncontrollable curiosity about its contents. It read:

MR MAAMUR
  I HOPE THAT YOU CAN HELP ME IN SEARCHING FOR WHOEVER OF MY FAMILY IS STILL ALIVE STOP I LEFT MY VILLAGE DARAWISH THIRTY YEARS AGO AT AGE TEN STOP GOD BLESSED ME OVER THE YEARS STOP I CAME TO PARIS AND BECAME WEALTHY STOP NOW FEEL A DEEP YEARNING TO SEE FAMILY AND HOME AND LEND A HELPING HAND IF I CAN STOP MY NAME IS HAMID MUSTAFA AL-BAHAIRI YOU WILL FIND MY FAMILY IS KNOWN IN DARAWISH STOP PLEASE SEND ALL INFORMATION I NEED AT ABOVE ADDRESS BY TELE-

GRAM TO ME AND HOPE WE WILL BECOME FRIENDS
WHEN WE MEET END

According to the dates on it, the telegram had been sent
from Paris a week ago and arrived in Cairo the same day
on which it was sent. I imagined that my successful and
rich fellow countryman was deeply worried by now and
possibly even becoming desperate. Normally, I would
have disregarded any such personal matter, falling as it
does outside the spheres of my professional or personal
obligations, but this matter seemed to me to be important, perhaps even urgent. Hamid Mustafa Al-Bahairi
was not an ordinary person. Surely here was a citizen
more deserving of my attention than any other. For me
his social status made him worthy of interest, especially
in my capacity as keeper of public safety.

I leaped from my chair and proceeded to attend
personally to this extraordinary matter; a matter in
which I felt I must be involved if only to secure the safety
of a person of note and to insure a safe and happy
outcome to the whole affair. Such a result would no
doubt help my own cause, too. I trusted no one else with
this affair. I could not send someone else to call on the
Omda of Darawish and acquire from him the needed
information. I ordered my soldier to prepare my official
private car and accompany me to Darawish. Soon, the
two of us and our driver were flying toward the village
over a pock-marked country road.

Mahmoud Ibn Al-Munsi

Suddenly, and with no warning, our world was turned upside-down before our very eyes, within our very minds. A stroke of fate fell unexpectedly, coming from the unknown, out of that dark and mysterious world beyond our vision and above our intellects. The sun still rose and set at its appointed time; the stars still came out at night, trailing after one another. Birds still fluttered their wings with the rise and set of the sun, and the tips of the trees and plants shook around us with each gust of wind. Babies had been born that morning, and people of all ages and both sexes had died, in our village and all neighboring villages, from As-Siyalla to Kafr Al-Liban.

Life went on as always. Bathwater and dishwater mixed with sweat and soap ran down the alleys and side-streets, spreading flies in its wake, and attracting the bills of ducks, hens' beaks, and geese. Donkeys brayed, dogs barked, and livestock clamored for their feed as children splashed in puddles of shallow water — flowing from the bodies of their bathing fathers — and from their mothers, who took their daughters up on the rooftops or in front of the houses and ran gasoline through their hair to kill lice and then combed it out with white or black combs made locally from animal bones. At each new dawn, the muezzin of the Mosque summoned the faithful to the dark and musty-smelling house of prayer following with the seasons the progress of the sun across the sky, and when, at night, some unknown stars shone, he announced the hours of darkness, of sleep, of sex and dreams. And then everything began again when, next morning, the women took off their soiled colored night clothes and dressed themselves in black for the day, and covered their heads and necks with light black shawls.

Everything happened just as it always had. Before this unexpected shock befell our village, everything had appeared natural in our eyes — familiar to our minds. This was life and there was no other life outside of it. It had accustomed us to people living and dying around us as well as to their hearty laughs and their faint groans, their careless smiles and concerned frowns. But now, even before anything tangible and material appeared for our eyes to inspect and our hands to grasp, we began to look toward this new awe-inspiring thing coming toward us, descending upon our village from above. We fell under its force in our feelings of backwardness and shame, our breathless anticipation, and our fear that we might see ourselves with new eyes. . . And that the Other might see us. That Other coming from a world ever unknown to us all, notwithstanding that small percentage of villagers who read the papers or peered through atlases and geography books with trachoma-stricken and night-blind eyes on the steps of the school classrooms in the nearest town. Now, I myself began to live with this new and coming thing. I awaited its arrival from Paris and forgot all possibility of my success or failure in the exams for my high school diploma. We could no longer have any conversation in our village unless it was about Hamid Ibn-Mustafa Al-Bahairi, our amazing and adventurous favorite son and worker of wonders.

We had been sitting at the coffeehouse near the bridge, playing cards, backgammon and dominoes. Buses, service cabs, horse-drawn carts, and private cars moved briskly past, heading north and south over the paved but cracked agricultural highway that was full of bumps and potholes and thirsting for a rinse and a new layer of asphalt. Then suddenly and unceremoniously, we found the messenger from the telegraph office pulling up beside us. Of course, by now we had already uttered under our breaths all the expectations, fantasies and dreams that could be whispered about Hamid Ibn-Mustafa Al-Bahairi. The messenger stepped off his bicycle and leaned it back on its stand. He extended an empty hand demanding a one pound tip from Ahmed Ibn-Mustafa Al-Bahairi, brother of Hamid and village greengrocer, who had left his shop in the care of his teenage son to come over and sit playing backgammon with us at the coffeehouse. Ahmed scoffed at the messenger until he defiantly waved the telegram in his other hand.

'It's a telegram for you from Paris, Mister Ahmed.'

'Paris?' Ahmed asked after swallowing hard.

He jumped up as though he were frightened. He appeared dazed, alarmed and giddy all at the same time. Snatching away the telegram anxiously, he opened it and ran his eyes impotently over its words, momentarily forgetting his virtual illiteracy. After a moment, he stopped and began threatening to beat the messenger to death for no apparent reason as we laughed and shouted in open mockery, 'Telegram! From Paris! For Ahmed Al-Bahairi?'

'Hand it to me,' I called out and proceeded to read it in a high voice while everyone listened silently as though we were in the presence of the Maamur or gathered before the prayer niche of the Mosque.

DEAR MOTHER BROTHER AHMED
    I AM ALIVE AND WELL STOP MARRIED WITH SON AND DAUGHTER STOP COMING TO VISIT YOU ALL BUT FOR ONLY TWO WEEKS DUE TO MUCH WORK HERE STOP AM SENDING TWO THOUSAND POUNDS BY TELEGRAM FOR CONSTRUCTION OF LARGE HOUSE NEAR BRIDGE IN CONSULTATION WITH ARCHITECT TO ACCOMMODATE MY PARISIAN WIFE DURING TWO WEEK STAY STOP YOU MAY PICK UP MONEY IMMEDIATELY AT TELEGRAPH OFFICE STOP I YEARN TO SEE YOU ALL AND SIMONE YEARNS TO MEET YOU STOP I THINK YOU WILL LOVE

HER MUCH AS SHE WILL LOVE YOU ESPECIALLY IF YOUR BEARING AND DEMEANOR TOWARD HER ARE GENTLE STOP UNTIL WE MEET MY DEARS. . .

One phrase hung in our minds and we all began to repeat it excitedly; 'I am sending you two thousand pounds'. We asked each other how two thousand pounds could possibly be sent like a wireless telegram. The messenger interrupted asking again for his due. Ahmed snatched the telegram from my hands and moved toward the doorway. He looked indescribably happy . . . not only about his brother but also about the two thousand pounds. When he seemed to be about to rush off to tell his mother the news, the messenger called after him again for his tip, even if it were only ten piastres. Ahmed stopped suddenly and stared for a moment, first toward town, then toward the bicycle, then came running back toward us shouting at the messenger to take him back into town while it was still mid-morning so he could claim his two thousand pounds before someone discovered a mistake in the telegram. The messenger protested at first, but when Ahmed promised to give him his pound upon claiming his money at the telegraph office, the messenger helped him onto the back of the bicycle and sped off with him toward the north, in the direction of the town.

Then, a gray old man, whom death had given a long reprieve, spoke thusly: 'Hamid Ibn-Mustafa stole five piastres thirty years ago from his father, God rest his soul. His deceased father at that time beat him and kicked him out of the house. . . The young man took it hard and never returned.'

But we were not really interested in wondering at the ways of the world. Something else was spinning in our minds. We were thinking of going and telling Hamid's mother the news. Except for a few people who were unconcerned by the matter or were just plain cold-hearted, the coffeehouse promptly emptied. We crowded through the doorway, in a rush.

For two whole weeks, the impending visit of Hamid and Simone would be uppermost in our minds.

Ahmed Al-Bahairi

I had never seen my brother's face. I was born several years after him according to my mother and the village elders. My mother, who had grown senile, and my father, who had died of dropsy, had found in me a replacement for that long lost son, and the others who'd died both before and after him.

Then the day came when telegrams began to arrive from my dear brother:

WE RODE STEAMER TODAY FROM TOULON PORT STOP AM ON WAY TO ALEXANDRIA WITH SIMONE TO CLAIM OUR PRIVATE CAR

ARRIVED ALEXANDRIA TODAY ON WAY TO CAIRO

WE ARE ON OUR WAY TO YOU AND WILL ARRIVE
TOMORROW AROUND NOON

The Maamur had sent a special messenger to invite
myself and the Omda to come to town, and we were
brought by the Maamur's private driver in his special
government car. There, the Maamur himself greeted us
— especially me — in an overly excited manner. We
started right away to talk about what should be done for
the reception of Simone and Hamid, to be sure of their
complete pleasure and comfort during their stay.

The Maamur insisted that I should make available
every sort of convenience and amusement for my brother
and his Parisian wife; and he made clear to me that the
house Hamid and Simone would stay in must have a
green garden with all types of jasmine and citrus trees
growing in it. He explained this could be done by
uprooting these, together with a few fig trees, and
replanting them in our garden as though they had been
growing there for a long time.

It was a shame that I couldn't build Hamid and
Simone the house they had asked for. The Architect told
me straight off it would take at least two months to build.
When we pressed him and even begged, he asked for a
huge sum of money as a settlement on the whole deal
which seemed to me far too much, and at any rate, was
more than Hamid had sent me.

No one in Darawish had ever consulted an architect before building a house. For this reason, the Omda and I and the other decision makers of our village found his services unnecessary. In fact, the village builders laughed at him. So we figured we'd build the house by ourselves, but then, even the workers of Darawish, whom we tried to line up to help, asked for double wages. They were probably just trying to take advantage of a once-in-a-lifetime opportunity. We didn't have much time and I'd already purchased for five hundred pounds a plot of land less than five hundred square metres.

My worries piled up. I couldn't sleep. I no longer knew day from night. Finally, before the Omda, the village elders, the night watchmen and their supervisor, the primary school teachers, high school students and community leaders, it was decided that renovation of the family house would be enough, and we asked the Maamur to approve our decision.

So I painted over the house with an oil-based paint. I bought new doors and fixed glass windows with screens. I also put down wood and tiles on the floor and installed a shower and a European toilet in the bathroom. I bought a new refrigerator and put a storage tank for water on the roof with pipes leading into the bathroom where I'd even fitted a washbasin for rinsing one's hands and face. The students from Darawish who were studying at the high school in the nearest town hung paintings they'd made on the walls after I put them in gilded frames. I covered the skylight in the roof with a pyramid of stained glass that had windows which opened and shut, and I pounded many nails and hooks into the walls of the bedrooms and living room in order to hang up gas lamps. And let's not forget the curtains, chairs, a dining-room table, bed spreads, white linen sheets, and towels for the kitchen and the bathroom.

This was all a big strain on me, financially as well as physically and, in the end, I didn't save any of the money I was sent. Whatever was left went to the tax collectors and go-betweens and the beady-eyed assessors who all began robbing me down to the last milleme — and even accused me to my face of theft, trickery, underestimation and all around penny-pinching. True, my shop did benefit from the money as did my house, but that was all part of my duty to create the comforts worthy of Simone. My shop had to look right for her, as it was a reflection upon our family. I painted its walls and shelves and replaced its façade, constructed glass counters, and decorated the shop front with Arabic inscriptions. All this had to be done. But the one problem that I could never solve were the flies that swarmed by day and the mosquitoes at night. When I sprayed disinfectant on a swarm, new swarms would replace it in an instant.

In the end I became angry and bitter about this visit, and about Hamid and Simone, who had stood our life (and the life of our whole village) on its head. But I swear, in spite of it all, that I was proud of my brother when I stood before the villagers of Darawish, and I swaggered among them, with my head raised boastfully, even more than the Omda himself strutting about with his whole entourage. Of course, I must admit that deep inside I felt jealousy toward Hamid and couldn't help but compare his money, his status and his wife, whom

I'd never laid eyes on, with my own money, status and wife. Finally, one night I saw myself killing Hamid in a dream — happily. I cried when I woke up out of disgust and self-hate, disgusted with the treacherous evil feelings in my heart. And I remembered the Mosque Imam, one radiant morning, telling us the story of Cain and Abel: I became scared that, one day, I would become that very man who'd killed his own brother out of jealousy.

The Omda

The Maamur had commended to me the need for Darawish to present a suitable appearance to Hamid. It was perhaps even more important that we impress his French wife Simone. That way, we would enable Hamid to raise his head proudly before his wife, and we in Darawish — and indeed all of Egypt — could raise our heads before foreigners as represented by the Lady Simone. I had promised the honorable Maamur that I would devote my full attention to overseeing the matter. I told him that I would call all Darawish's village elders to an emergency meeting. I then returned to Darawish after my encounter with the Maamur, and ever since then the entire village has been in a state of emergency, preparing to welcome Hamid Ibn Mustafa Al-Bahairi, whom God blessed in the foreign lands, and who would bring with him his wife, Simone, who was French and European: a stranger.

I told everyone that Darawish must present an appearance worthy of itself and the Egyptian mother-land. They all agreed and we began over the course of the next two weeks to trim the grass along the canals, to repair the bridges (in case Lady Simone wished to walk over them some afternoon), and to fill up the puddles and swamps with earth. We felt lucky that there were no rice fields near Darawish since they attract mosquitoes to the streets and houses. We improved the village's roads and filled their potholes with rubble left over from the repaving of the bridges bordering the fields. We also made a deal with a store in the nearby town on the purchase of a number of lamps which we would set up at the first opportunity on the corners of the main streets of the village for as many nights as Simone stayed in Darawish to give her the impression that our streets had been lit every night for years. We further agreed upon the need to cover the main streets with sand borne by camels and donkeys, after having been brought by rented dump trucks, from the desert on the opposite bank of the river. We even reserved a small cabin at a nearby summer resort for Simone to stay in for a day or more if she liked.

I issued an order, which I circulated through the village criers, forbidding the throwing out of dishwater in the back alleys and side-streets. I made clear that anyone disobeying this order would be subject to severe punishment at the hands of the Omda of the village and the Maamur of the town, and that it was the responsibility of the villagers present to inform anyone temporarily away from the village to obey the order. Finally, to be extra safe, I commanded the watchmen of the village (as well as the villagers themselves) to keep the dung from livestock and mules off the streets of Darawish, day and night, and I impressed upon these same watchmen the importance of their keeping a look-out for village children so that they didn't piss in the streets or behind houses.

We exhausted ourselves for two whole weeks carrying out what we'd agreed upon and overseeing the completion of renovations and clean-ups. We spent the few nights leading up to the couple's arrival sitting in a village hall talking about what we had done and what we still needed to do — but these discussions always included various stories of Simone's French homeland.

Some of the teachers present at the gathering would remind us, for example, of our wars with the French that were fought over a hundred and fifty years ago. Among them was a story I remembered being told by my grandparents, God rest their souls. It was that the French had settled in Darawish for several years during Napoleon's invasion and even lived in sin (God save us from such depravity) with the women of the village. Some of them stayed in our country after the French army left, converted to Islam and married our daughters, then worked as traders or farmed the land. We also learned from our cherished and honorable elders, who had in turn learned it from their deceased forefathers, that seventeen thousand villagers of Darawish and the surrounding area had died at the hands of Simone's ancestors. We were all extremely upset and angry about this fact, but we decided with the guidance of the Mosque Iman that the requirement of blood vengeance against Simone's people had dissipated completely with the passing of seven generations. In the end, we laughed together that all this had led us to discover the secret behind the elegant whiteness of the complexions of our women as well as the secret behind the large proportion of children with light-coloured eyes, not only in Darawish, but in the whole surrounding area, from Farskour to Azbt-al-Borg and from Port Said to Alexandria.

It was my estimate, as I'm sure it was the estimate of the others (even though none would dare say it), that Hamid was now the possessor of ample riches and property. He had to return to Darawish, his motherland, where he'd been born and rested his head as a child; and — for his wife's sake at the very least — he could not bear a grudge against his village which had already paid such a price for losing him. He had to raise his head high and lift the collective head of Darawish before the whole of the outside world. We had to make the visit something Simone would talk about when she returned to her country, happy and healthy and remembering fondly our simple yet beautiful village, sitting like a shining bride near the bend of the river.

Mahmoud Ibn Al-Munsi

Finally, the great day arrived. The women of the village awoke early and adorned both themselves and their sons and daughters in their finest clothes. All the boys and girls came out of their homes decked out for a magnificent holiday. True, their clothes were old; but with the break of that day they were all cleaned and patched with stitches sewn with precision and care. Most of them had no shoes; but their feet had been carefully washed and dried by a mother or older sister before they left the house. The men, particularly the prominent figures, the fancy dressers and village elders, all wore clothes that were clean and, in some instances, even pressed in the nearby town. As for the women, especially those who were married or over thirty, they wore their normal black clothes and covered their heads with the traditional shawl, despite the extreme heat.

Of course, the affair did meet some indifference as well, from many of the men and women of the village. They began going about their normal daily routine; working in their homes, along the roads and in the fields. But these people were of no importance. They were not prominent or notable figures in the village. Why else would they have labored away as they did every day to bring home their daily bread?

As the noon hour approached, our village's beautiful façade began to crumble. People in the coffeehouse scraped at the shape and shine of their shoes and messed up clothes, victims of the heat, perspiration and just plain neglect. After a long period of restraint, the boys and girls began playing games, soiling their clothes, shoes and feet. The smooth sand-covered surfaces of the streets — especially the one leading to Ahmed Al-Bahairi's house — got covered with dirt and animal droppings with the villagers, old and young moving about as well as the bicycles, carts and automobiles. Swarms of flies and their noisey humming also increased with the heat as the noon hour approached, particularly in areas shaded by trees or walls.

As the promised hour neared, a crowd began to gather along the paved agricultural highway. The chairs in the coffeehouse were abandoned, and many villagers sought shade under the few scattered trees, pavillions and walls surrounding the fields. As time passed, the traffic near the farm fields increased, and the workers began to sit down or squat in the fields to watch and wait. The rooftops of the houses, from the opposite bank of the river to the small canal, began to fill with women standing or sitting, some plopped down on piles of wood or straw, gathering up the ends of their head scarves to shield themselves against the intense heat of the scorching sun. The watchmen scattered here and there keeping the children in line behind the archway in front of the village.

Some waited quietly, but in general, whispered conversations and tall tales increased as the blazing sun rose up into the pure, chalky heavens. Most eyes were gazing intensely toward the south where they hoped to catch a glimpse of Hamid Al-Bahairi's Parisian car. Then, suddenly, in a dazzling moment I'll never forget, the car appeared, darting around the curve at the Adilia traffic point.

There the Maamur and officers, along with the Omda of the village and prominent figures from both the town and the village, were waiting to meet Simone and Hamid Al-Bahairi; and from that point all the way to the village entrance and beyond, over one hundred soldiers stood dreaming of being blessed by Hamid Al-Bahairi.

Then, at long last . . . that unforgettable moment arrived. The noon's brilliant light, sparkling through the leaves of the trees, fell on to the car's red chassis as it stopped abruptly at the traffic point. Everyone — adults and children — charged. The soldiers from the town and the watchmen forgot about their duties and raced toward the red car. Even those still working in their fields and houses rushed out, overcome by their curiosity, leaving behind them tools, livestock or dirty dishes. A roar rose above the women's ululations and the children's screams of joy: It's Hamid! Hamid and the French Madame.

If King Farouk himself had been coming to call, there wouldn't have been such a scene. The stampede of people stirred up a cloud of flying dust, which dissipated as the people slowly drew back in advance of the car, slowing its forward progress. Oncoming traffic, heading toward the town, was stopped by the crowd, but its honking horns of protest became rhythmic chants of welcome once the drivers learned from the waiter at the coffeehouse what was happening. Birds taking refuge from the heat among the tree branches were startled by the noise and took flight in all directions over the heads of the villagers. In spite of the car's slowness, the notables from the town and the village and the soldiers broke into a run beside and behind the procession, as did the villagers. The horns of the two cars carrying the Maamur and the officers bellowed warnings to the crowd, and the prominent wide red car led the way surrounded by a squadron of parade motorcycles commandeered especially for such occasions.

The length of the wait had affected me, and what I was now seeing stunned me as I stood frozen on the bridge at the entrance to the village, momentarily forgetting my charge to stay near Simone whenever she was with the Omda or Ahmed Al-Bahairi because of my knowledge of her native tongue. The car approached the bridge as the people around it pushed and shoved, and then, in a flash, I saw the two worlds before me: the faces of the mob and the faces of Simone and her husband, whose bearing and even skin color had changed much, to the point that you could no longer tell he was from Darawish stock, even though there had been a time when he was one of its barefoot children in tattered clothes complaining constantly of cramps, headaches, dizziness, red urine and eye sores. And he would have remained one of us, had he been fated to live out his life in Darawish.

The plan had been for the wide red car to be driven over the bridge, but the narrow main street would have stopped it from going any further. Hamid must have noticed the problem, because he steered his car off to the right while the soldiers beat the people back, and parked it in an open space that he seemed to remember between the coffeehouse and the tin structure containing the village mill. He then stepped down from the car, while she remained seated. He circled around to open the door for her, but the Maamur was quicker. He opened the door, then bent down and said to her in heavily accented French:

'Bienvenue.'

Then Simone stepped down.

So, this was Simone. Coming fresh from the City of Lights, from the land of grand boulevards and the famous Sorbonne, the Latin Quarter, the Bois de Boulogne and the Champs-Elysées. The Maamur walked in front of her clearing the way as she followed with Hamid, followed in turn by the officers, then the Omda, then the elders. Hamid was relentlessly elegant. Health poured out of him. His stoutness showed clearly on his large

frame. As for Simone, she wasn't really so appealing . . .
neither particularly beautiful nor ugly. Her skin was red
having been quickly scorched by the sun along the way.
Her narrow frame was full and tender. Her complexion
and her blue patterned dress were enchanting together.
She had a light gait and sparkling blue eyes full of life.
There were many women in the village more attractive
and appealing than she was, but she had a certain spirit
about her, a self-confidence and strength. There was a
lightness and mirth exuding from her, and I felt sorry for
all our women when I compared them to her.

We all crossed the bridge behind the leaders, trying to
see what we could of the goings on of this rare occasion, a
Frenchwoman in Darawish. . . Ah, Simone. What a
beautiful and magical name! The beauty of her eyes!
And the magic of that camera, hung around her shoulders, dangling at her slender waist.

TUMULT IN DARAWISH

Hamid Al-Bahairi

The joy of returning to my homeland dissipated like a dream evaporating with the shock of waking. While we were still in Alexandria, and even to some extent Cairo, this world seemed somewhat like the one we knew. The buildings and paved roads were like those we'd left behind in Paris, Nice, and Deauville. But life's daily routine differed greatly as did the people I'd left behind me in France and those I saw before me in Egypt. Although most of the people were bareheaded with neatly combed hair, some wore fezzes or turbans. They wore both native and European dress, including a number of business suits. They often bore a resemblance to

Simone's countrymen, in spite of their brown faces and dark eyes. But the culture and spirit of the place! The difference in standards of cleanliness and mentality!

The conduct of bureaucrats, clerks, porters and peddlers was extremely annoying, both for myself and others. I attributed this to the heat, perspiration, flies and the dust, whose particles rose up and blanketed everything they touched. But whether it was justified or not, my heart was not at peace with the pungent smells of the spices, the language of the foulmouths around us, and the general lack of grace and polish.

I kept looking toward Simone to catch her reaction to my country and its people in her facial expressions or in her liquid eyes. But her joy over the voyage and its adventures reigned, enabling her to bear anything with the patience of a camel. I was aware that this was happening to her, in spite of my own wild craving to see my family and village, and the canal and the bridge at the village entrance, and the date palms and ancient sycamore trees. Could it all still be there? I had carried their names inside myself, and their images — misty, vague, anchorless — had piled themselves upon me and been lodged in the caverns of my distant memories, constantly twisting and torturing me when I tried to sleep, whether on the deck of a Mediterranean steamer or on a train in Europe, or at work in a mine or a restaurant, or presiding, finally, over one of my elegant shops or my famous Parisian hotel.

Along the way, I stopped seeing any resemblance to Europe's forests, farms and rich, terraced verdure. Our car rocked back and forth in spasms, and dirt spewing out from beneath its wheels drifted back over us, leaving its residue on the clinging perspiration that covered us and its smell in our noses. Green trees — scrawny, scraggly, and sick-looking — lined the sides of the road along with the telephone poles, the modest farms and the canal. It bothered me that the peasants in the fields still did their work mostly with their hands, alongside their mules, cattle and water buffalo, just as it bothered me to see the villages full of low adjoining mud structures and brown faces — shrivelled, stark and wan — proclaiming their own anemia, dysentery and vitamin deficiency . . . and I said to myself:

'So this is my country.'

The amazing thing was that Simone was delighted by what she was seeing. The bright scorching sun, the vegetation and the primitive life all pleased her, and every so often she would cry out: 'Oh Hamid! Look! . . . What a quaint land! . . . All this water . . . Is your country always flooded with sunlight even in winter. Doesn't it ever snow?'

But she would also ask:

'Where are the forests? Why does everyone look sick? Why don't the people use machinery in their farming? Why do the children all walk around barefoot?'

Her questions killed me, and I kept repeating to myself,

'This is my homeland. These are my people.'

She would notice the embarrassment on my face and would then say to me with that famous and sensitive politeness of her people: '*Pardon, mon chéri.*' Then she would go back to asking questions and taking pictures.

How I wished she had taken no pictures at all of these sights that I found so humiliating. They would neither help me nor honor me in Paris. *Mais c' était là la vérité de ce pays.* That's the way it is, and there's no way around it.

We were stopped several times on the road by the police, but my knowledge of Arabic and the papers I carried from Cairo helped me greatly, my foreign accent and French passport notwithstanding. I was constantly forced to explain the reason for my travels in Egypt. At one of the stops, as we passed through a village called Kufr Shakr, Simone wanted to stop and drink something at the village's modest coffeehouse and to buy fresh fruit to eat as we sat. We turned our car around and drove back up the road a few metres, then stopped beside the road and got out. Simone washed her arms and face and we drank a couple of sodas that were barely refrigerated. The owner of the coffeehouse washed the fruit himself before we ate it. Eventually, several villagers, including women and children, formed a ring around us, as though we had just come from another planet. Then we resumed our journey.

Along the way, I feared that she would be stricken with cramps caused by the peaches and apricots that she'd eaten, which, I was sure, had been washed with canal water. . . Or even that I myself might be stricken, if not by cramps then by dysentery. Surely, I'd never forget those ten years I'd spent here and the pain that had been a large part of it. I'd learned the reasons for these illnesses in Paris, but that didn't save me from continuing to suffer from them years later.

When we arrived at the Adilia crossroad and I saw the

policemen, I thought at first that there was some problem. When I realized the truth, I was irritated by the elaborate reception. Maybe it was because I was embarrassed in front of Simone for my family and for the officials, peasants and children. That was the cause of the irritation that I hid in my heart behind my broad smile, especially when I saw the happiness in Simone's face.

Here was my brother, whom I had yearned to embrace for so long, and there was my skinny old mother, who had shrunk in height and weight over the years. I greeted them and let them kiss me. My mother hugged Simone and kissed her on both cheeks, then began feeling up her hair and arms in front of everyone, to Simone's surprise. Then she fired into the air a long, shrill and hoarse ululation that could only be stopped by a sudden hacking cough.

This was my village: Darawish, with its low mud buildings and narrow streets as though it were in constant fear of a coming invasion, the blackness covering people's faces and coloring women's clothes; it's dried and dusty salt marshes and its piles of hay on the rooftops. This was the dream that I'd lived, been pulled by, come back for. In spite of it all, it was lodged in my heart, raging and storming, and I felt along with my irritation and disgust, a love and a peace. I thought: is Simone really pleased with what she sees, hears and smells? I asked her, and she answered, nodding her head as her eyes sparkled with a deep content: '*Beaucoup!*'

But I was aware even then that this euphoria would soon disappear, leaving behind a bad taste in our mouths behind it, and I was annoyed to the extreme when, just before I parked the car by the coffeehouse, my brother Ahmed told me he hadn't been able to build us a house by the agricultural highway. But I gave in to the circumstances, once he'd assured me that our old home (that I remembered as being dark and gloomy and surrounded on three sides by a poor neighborhood) had been restored to a splendor that would please Simone.

And the excitement of the people swelled all around us as though I were a conquering hero, returning victoriously from a horrible war with my car and with my European wife, Simone; and I thought, if only someone would present her with a bouquet of flowers, or even a modest green plant pulled from this noble earth.

Ahmed Al-Bahairi

Simone walked out of the bathroom that first morning with her wet hair dangling around her shoulders like a mermaid and went into her bedroom. My wife, Zeinab, and I had moved out of the same room a few days earlier and crowded in with my mother for the sake of our two guests of honor. Hamid then went into the bathroom and came out after a while to catch up with Simone. When they emerged from their room they were all dressed up (which amazed me since it was morning and they weren't going anywhere). Simone had on a short gray dress and Hamid wore a blue suit and necktie. Like the waiter at the Nahar Coffeehouse in the town. We had put our fancy plates out on the lunch table, and there was so much food we could have fed the entire neighborhood. It was so much that it made Simone scream with amazement. Then she calmed down and began to chatter in her own tongue about the generosity of the East and the waste and folly of it all. I swear to God, that's what Hamid told us she was saying. I was amazed by her orders as we sat at the table: 'Soup first, then the other dishes, one after the other.' It was bizarre. She had to force her own way on the rest of us through Hamid, who translated for us what she wanted, repeating her remarks one by one, at the same time telling me that a person should eat and drink the way the people do in the country he visits.

I tried to make Simone laugh during the lunch, but when Hamid would relay to her what I'd said in his stuffy, formal way, she would just smile and say: 'Bravo.'

Honestly, I was embarrassed about my appearance next to Hamid's, and Zeinab's next to Simone's, and we won't even mention my mother. The village tailor had tried to cut me a cashmere suit that made me sweat buckets in that heat and over that hot bowl of soup. The seamstress, Rafraf, had also done all she could to see that my mother and wife were smartly dressed, but all her work just made them look funny.

Every now and then, I would forget myself while drinking my soup and make a loud slurping sound, even though I myself had warned my wife and my mother about not doing just that. My mother, of course, constantly fell into this same trap. Zeinab, on the other hand, didn't forget even once and never stopped looking at mother and me with disapproval. She watched carefully whatever Simone did at the table and tried to do likewise, whether it was the raising of the spoon or the setting it down, or even the extent to which she opened her mouth before putting the food into it. But she really did look strange when she tried to use her knife the way Simone did, and I thought to myself that human beings just can't change their habits overnight.

Then, when Simone stuck her arm out to stab the turkey leg with her knife, she exposed the long yellow hairs in her armpits. I felt disgusted. My wife realized what I had seen and smiled sarcastically and stared at me. I leered back at her in anger, afraid that Hamid might notice the silent conversation passing between us. It struck me that beauty can never be fully perfected, as I wondered at how Simone could neglect her bodily hygiene so much, being the civilized, elegant woman that she was, and knowing that she was going to visit her husband's family in a strange and foreign land.

Hamid and Simone were eating in small bites and practically whispered when they spoke, so that my mother, who was hard of hearing, kept leaning her ear toward me and asking in a loud voice what they were saying. Hamid would try to raise his voice a little and answer her patiently in broken spaced-out phrases as though he were trying to search for words that he'd forgotten over the course of thirty years of exile: words that he needed me to remind him of. Now and then he would even stick a French word in in the middle of his sentences, causing my mother to open her mouth in shock, while Zeinab tried to suppress a laugh, and

Hamid stared back at them both, equally amazed.

We finished the meal, then Hamid and I went into the living quarter. Simone insisted on staying behind to help my mother and Zeinab and the servant we had rented for a few days to help out, to give Simone a good impression. Hamid took a small notebook from his pocket, as soon as we were alone. He asked me if any of the money he'd sent was left over, and I told him all the different things I'd spent it on. Strangely enough, he wasn't upset that it had been used up, and in fact, gave me another 100 pounds to spend while he was with us. He then settled into a long conversation in which he asked me about my work and overall situation. He wanted to know about our father's final days. Then he began asking about our relatives, family by family, and even person by person: who had been born, who had married, who had had children, who had died, who had moved away and who had stayed behind. He would ask these things, then listen to me silently writing away from the left of the page to the right, putting down numbers. I was too embarrassed to try to sneak a look. He took out his wallet again and put it in front of himself, then he pulled a long, fat, brown cigar out of a case, lit it and gave it to me. Then he pulled out another just like it which he put in his mouth and lit as he began counting out money: 'This is for so and so . . . and this is for so and so,' etc. And I said to myself, as I considered the money and cigar, that here was really a man of noble deeds who let no chance to be generous pass him by. Yes, he never forgot even a small act of kindness; but to tell the truth, I thought he was crazy because he was flinging all this money at us and rousing our envy. A tenth of the amount would have been enough to make our eyes bulge, since they bulged at anything that was much more than plain dirt. Besides, I was his own brother and I could have, with this money alone, bought fertilizer, rice, wheat, gasoline, seeds, cotton, fabrics . . . everything imaginable. So I decided to myself that I would carry out his instructions in my own way. After all, I understood things here better than he did, and my mother, my children and I were his closest relatives and should have been the first to gain from his spendthrift ways.

While we sat together, my children came from their Aunt's — the three boys and the two girls — and I introduced them to him. They said hello and kissed him, and he tossed each of them five pounds and began to chat with them. With a touch of reproach he told me that the two girls had to begin going to school in the town, and I pretended to agree with him. He said I should send him a letter in Paris to tell him when any of them were about to get married and also to let him know when my oldest son was about to graduate from high school so that he could arrange for him to complete his higher education in Paris. For that I felt so obliged to him that tears began rolling down my cheeks and I thanked him deeply, calling on God to shower him with blessings, until he stopped me with a wave of his hand and the comment that it was his duty since he was my brother.

Then my mother, Zeinab and Simone came in, and Simone screamed again when she saw my children and kissed them. She tried (foolishly) to speak to them, but, of course, they didn't understand. I started to feel their visit had gone on long enough, so I motioned to them with my eyes to leave. Simone caught what I'd done and seemed to me to disapprove, but the children, who usually do what I say, got up and said goodbye anyway and left to go back to their Aunt's. I excused myself for a moment as well, then went out behind them and took away the money they'd been given. Of course, I did this so they wouldn't lose it, or give it to Zeinab who might take it on some pretext. But I warned them anyway not to say anything to their Aunt about the money before I went back to the living quarter.

Our visit went on a while longer until I noticed Simone caressing Hamid's hair, and I thought to myself that she probably wanted him, right then. My mother was staring and laughing, while Zeinab stole glances in their direction, and I worried that one of them might do something improper. So I got up and excused myself, taking with me my mother and Zeinab, and Hamid accompanied his wife to their room so they could both rest a little.

I found myself wanting Zeinab, even after such a heavy meal. But my mother, whom we'd been sharing a room with for the past two weeks, didn't catch on. Eventually, we managed to lure her up to the roof to feed and look after the chickens until sunset.

It never occurred to me that as my pleasure with Zeinab rose I would feel as though I was holding Simone tightly in my arms, and I noticed that Zeinab also was meeting me with a passion I hadn't seen in years.

The Omda

had prepared an unforgettable evening. We laid down
rugs on the balcony, in the reception parlor and in the
guest hall and mats in the courtyard. We'd hung dozens
of lamps which lit up the residence at night as though we
were in the middle of the afternoon. The furniture shop
in the town had supplied the entire place with the finest
articles. The walls were lined with tapestries embroi-
dered by the tent maker, and more furniture and mats in
the courtyard had been added, as were trays, plates and
silverware, and generally everything required for an
evening of high culture, the like of which had never
occurred in our district.

Then we all waited: the Maamur, the town elders, the officers, the elders of Darawish and myself. Simone, Ahmed, and his brother Hamid arrived together. Her appearance pleased me as a red blooded male, but angered me as a gentleman. Her back was bare down to below her shoulders. Her hair hung down over her long neck that looked like a gazelle's. Her two breasts stood firm and round with the cleavage between them disgracefully exposed. She wore a short red dress cut above her knees which made all the young men, who'd gathered outside the hall from Darawish and all the surrounding area, cheer like crazy people. I thought to myself she would surely corrupt them and end up charming us away from our black-clad women and our modest and virtuous young girls.

But what could one do? That's the way things were in her country, and one must finish what one starts. After all, she was a guest and the wife of one of Darawish's native sons, even if the scene made me look down on Hamid himself and lowered him in my esteem, causing me to whisper to myself secretly: 'Shameless bastard.'

Of course, Simone was the only woman in the room except for the belly dancer; after all, what villager would bring his wife to such a place? No one from the town — neither the Maamur, the officers, the Town Doctor, the Agricultural Engineer, nor the Inspector of Supplies — brought theirs. We all sat at one table and all the elders sat at the tables around us. (The Maamur himself had arranged the seating.) He seated Simone at the head of the table with himself on her immediate left directly across from her husband, while I sat facing Simone at the other end of the table. But when I tried to tease him about sitting next to her he just said:

'It's all by rank, Mr Omda.'

Loud noises came in from outside the hall as the watchmen and soldiers armed with nightsticks faced a crowd of women, children and youngsters all enchanted by Simone. A store in town had solved our silverware problem by providing us with large packages of knives and forks so that we didn't fall into the same trap as Ahmed Al-Bahairi had done when he realized, as he prepared for their arrival, that there wasn't a single fork in all of Darawish. Simone, of course, started to eat with her knife and fork with the utmost skill, never injuring herself once with the teeth of the fork or with that sharp knife blade that could slice a piece of meat in two at a mere touch. Hamid did likewise and the Maamur, officers, Doctor and Engineer followed suit.

As for Ahmed Al-Bahairi and myself, everyone must have noticed that our attempts to eat like them were tortuous. In the end, I don't remember eating anything much at all since I didn't want to make a fool of myself in front of Simone. I tried to conceal my ignorance behind a pretext of being a moderate eater in any case, who was satisfied by the generosity and bounty piled upon the surprised and delighted Simone. I even, for good measure, leered at the gluttonous Maamur and the elders several times as they made loud noises while drinking their water and soup. This seemed to me inappropriate in Simone's presence. They would break in two with their hands pieces of chicken or pigeon dripping with grease. They would fill their faces with food, then chew, then burp. They continued taking second helpings, too, and God knows, they weren't paying a milleme for any of it. God save anyone who tries to be generous to them. People's minds close once their stomachs are opened.

Simone, herself, didn't eat much. She wiped the sides of her mouth with the napkin after a while and declined to wash her hands and mouth, waiting instead in her chair for everyone to finish their meal until, finally, the Maamur and myself convinced her that she didn't have to wait any longer. She got up and we got up with her: the Maamur, his lackeys, Hamid, Ahmed and myself, that is, while all the others remained seated trying to fill their bottomless stomachs, which they'd apparently not put anything into all day.

We took her out onto the balcony which we'd furnished with rugs and plush couches, and she sat with Hamid in the place of honor. Then she began fanning herself with a delicate colored fan like the ones I'd seen a few times before carried by beautiful women in the cabarets of Cairo. She covered her shoulders with a shawl to protect herself against the flies, moths and mosquitoes swarming around the gas lamps, so I tried to apologize to her through Mahmoud Ibn Al-Munsi (that accomplished student, whose father was an overseer in the fields). But Hamid dismissed the matter. He told us that they had prepared for the problem by covering their skin with a special oil so that flies and mosquitoes would not come near them and annoy them. And I said to myself, surely these people possess knowledge above us all.

Glasses of mango juice were passed around followed

by a round of coffee and tea, and some of the men began cane fencing in the middle of the courtyard. Then Ibrahim, the village singer, began singing a Mawwail about love to the accompaniment of a wooden flute. Then a gypsy dancer, whom we'd brought in for just such a moment, entered and began to dance to the music of the flute, a tar drum and a tambourine. At about that time Simone began chatting with a few of the officers who knew the language of her country; which by the way, one of them had even visited and stayed in for a year. She also talked on the topic of singers in France with Mahmoud Ibn Al-Munsi, who knew much about her country even though he had never visited it.

Hamid (whose name Simone had trouble pronouncing) was very generous with us. He left Simone on the balcony to watch and chat and take dozens of pictures, and he invited the Maamur and myself into an adjoining room and gave him hundreds of pounds for his policemen (God knows how much of it they'll really see) and gave me money as well for the watchmen and improvements in Darawish and for the price of the reception, which was really only about a sixth of the amount Hamid had given me. But he did also ask me to pass some out as charity for the poor of Darawish who gathered and danced and hung on the walls outside, in the darkness cut only by the shining lamps inside, yelling and chanting and calling for Hamid to have a long and prosperous life with his beautiful French Madame.

What Hamid Ibn-Mustafa Al-Bahairi paid out that day was enough to purchase several acres of land even in this time of rising land and cotton prices, and I began to look at him as a bearer of many blessings who distributed good luck among our people. At that moment, I felt I understood what the Mosque Imam had meant when he'd said: 'Perhaps what you despise is actually best for you.' Amen. Hamid had left our land an exiled vagrant, then returned from across the seven seas a revered conqueror, like Sindbad whom Ibrahim sang about. I began to wish that Hamid would stay with us forever, and I almost told him of my wish, but then I became fearful of calling his attention to an idea he had never had and which might actually cause him to stay with us here in Darawish. I was afraid he might become a challenger to me or that he might raise the very modest level of his family through his status and his wealth to the level of my own. I was confused: did I love Hamid or hate him? I was amazed by God's decrees, His will, and His mysterious ways. I had been the biggest man in Darawish when, suddenly, the son of Al-Bahairi showed up to make me realize that he was even bigger. My family was the richest family in Darawish and from the finest stock; then along came Al-Bahairi's son to make his family finer with his money, his status, and his French wife, whose appearance left us with no doubt about her. . . May God who honored the son of Adam by making him in His image save our souls.

The party concluded that night without incident. Simone took dozens of pictures, including a picture of me which she said would come out in color, and she promised to send me a copy of it from Paris. Then everyone went back to their houses to rest, but dreams of Simone stayed with me. I saw her once as a 'Houri' or

Virgin of Paradise, and another time as a Genie rising out of the sea, whose enchanting power over Darawish, in the company of her husband Hamid, exceeded that of Satan. Later that night, my wife came toward me uncharacteristically made up, wearing more perfume than she had on our wedding night. After twenty-five years of marriage! I shouted at her then turned my back to her, and I don't think I'd be lying to myself if I said at that moment that I felt as though she were a cow . . . a mere cow.

Then the phantom of Hamid himself came to me and made me think to myself, as I floated toward that small death called sleep, who am I in comparison to him? The thought came to me as I tried to sleep, in spite of all my anxiety. I began thinking about what I would do with Hamid's money. Suddenly, I found myself calling on God to save me from the enchanting powers of Simone from the land of the Franks, who appeared to my mind's eye like a Genie from the Garden of Eden.

Ahmed Al-Bahairi

Just by coming to our village and staying in my house Hamid and Simone hurt me a great deal. I can't help but remember how the devilish children of Darawish suddenly began to delight in pissing against our house, until the Omda finally had to send a watchman to guard us all night. Those same devilish children broke the glass and the mantel of the lamps hanging on the street corners, so that Darawish returned to its old familiar darkness.

Also, it seemed to me that Zeinab had fallen for Hamid and that she was practically competing with Simone in being close to him, smiling at him, jumping to serve him and dolling herself up for his sake. It had to be true. Zeinab was starting to mispronounce Hamid's name the same way Simone did and she would say things to him like:

'*Oo* . . . '*Amid* . . . *pardon* . . . *Monsieur Hamid* . . . *merci. . .*'

She even started answering Simone's comments and questions with: '*Oui, Madame,*' although she never understood what Simone was saying to her.

Even when we were alone together in our room, after Simone had trimmed Zeinab's hair, she started saying to me: '*Pardon, mon chéri, Monsieur 'Ahmed.*'

Things went so far that one night, for the first time ever, she refused me, using the excuse that she was tired and not in the mood and adding that she had grown tired of our behaving like a couple of rabbits. Then, when I made the mistake of trying to coax her, she said to me:

'So she's got you hot has she?'

'Who?'

'Her . . . shall I call her for you?'

I was on the point of coming at her with a cane, to beat her and not stop until she remembered her manners just as I had the day she claimed to be possessed by an evil spirit who wanted to scream through her. How badly I wanted to slap her face until it bled whenever she mispronounced my name by saying it with a French accent. But to tell the truth, I was frightened that Simone would disapprove. I dreaded her being angry with me or that Hamid would look down on me with disgust. My mother would cackle like a spirit from the dead whenever she saw Zeinab and me at odds, and we'd end up escaping to the roof to try to come to some understanding and to sleep in the open air. When I did finally manage to coax Zeinab into it, she felt to me as cold as a tile floor in winter. I was unbearable even to myself, engaging in a private routine wearily and with effort until, in the end, I would turn my back to her unfeelingly, without saying a word. But I would be unable to sleep all night until the roosters crowed and the donkeys brayed and the dogs finally stopped their nocturnal barking.

I thought later that if Zeinab really feared that I fancied Simone to the point of being in love with her, she might stop being so interested in Hamid. So I tried to play that part with Simone in front of Zeinab in order to keep her by making her jealous: but she never did anything to give away her jealousy. She was only jealous of the love Hamid felt for Simone, but she mocked me because she knew from the start that someone like Simone would never pay any attention to me. Once she even insulted me by saying I wasn't like Hamid, and that time I did slap her hard on the face. But she didn't cry out at all. She just walked out angrily and sat by herself in the living quarter trying to pick up the sounds coming from behind the closed door of Hamid and Simone's room. My mother meanwhile began to look more feeble-minded than ever. Every afternoon she would try to force us all to take a nap — even Simone who had once told us that she never slept during the day. She would also stretch out on her stomach on the roof of the house and, hanging her head over the edge, call out to people walking in the street to come in to our house and eat with us. She told them we had lots of food and even threw some of it out every day to the chickens, who'd grown used to eating meat since they never ate anything else anymore. They had become voracious, she would say, and would end up eating each other once it came time to return to our old ways of being poor and empty-handed. I would listen to my mother and try to pretend she was talking to herself out loud. But I was also scared that Hamid would hear her (in spite of how far away from her his room was) if he ever opened up his window to the fields filled with date palms and other trees. So I went up on the roof to try and bring my mother back to her senses with a mixture of anger and softness so that Simone wouldn't get the idea, for example, that she was crazy. When I said this, my mother screamed at me, as though Simone had actually said that to her face, shouting: 'So I'm crazy, Simone. Fine! You daughter of red demons. By God, I won't let her stay in my house, or let him stay with her for one more minute, I'll throw her out.'

'Mother, I didn't mean it. Simone never really said it, but she could be thinking it.'

Then she pushed me away and went back to her bed in the shade of the wall of the hen house, where she folded herself up and began to tremble as though she were crying for someone.

Hamid also confused and distressed me. I told myself he was my brother and I was proud of him , and said so before the people. He had raised my status in Darawish and in the town. He had provided some fame to my formerly unknown shop, which was run for the time being by my oldest son. But I didn't feel like he was really my brother. I searched but could not find a single childhood memory that we'd shared together. He was still a stranger to me. I was not like my mother who remembered everything he did, and always had another story to tell about things that happened to him during those ten years he'd lived in Darawish. As far as I knew, none of it had ever happened. But she never grew tired of reminding him of these things or relating them to the neighbors and the elders of the village. She assured them all, for instance, that she had known he would be lucky ever since he was a year old. It began to seem to me that my mother really had gone crazy, but Zeinab was ten times worse.

One day I came back to the house from my shop after a quick review of the business. It was dusk and women were sitting around on the roofs of the nearby houses sewing, and there were children listening quietly with open mouths and staring toward the closed door of our house. I hurried until I was close enough to hear foreign music bursting out from the middle of our house. I chased away the children and waved at the women to go back inside their own houses. I went inside and slammed the door behind me, without giving myself a chance to see how they had ignored my orders. Hamid's door was closed, and the music coming from the room was shaking the walls slightly. Meanwhile, my mother was peeking through the keyhole while Zeinab tried to push her away to take her own turn to look. I shouted at them, and they moved away toward the middle of the living room. Then I drew near the door myself and looked through its keyhole. They were dancing together.

At that moment, I didn't know my head from my feet. The scene pleased, excited and angered me all at once. When I turned to fume at Zeinab and my mother, I found Zeinab, dancing with her two hands grasping her own arms in imitation of Simone's embrace of Hamid, while my mother laughed with delight. Great God! Zeinab was in a dream. Dreaming with him and about him. I lost my senses and began looking around for something to strike her in the face with, but the two of them escaped quickly into our room and locked the door behind them.

I sighed in anger and waited for a moment, then leaned back down to the keyhole to see Simone as she moved lightly with Hamid, neither of them ever stepping on the other's feet. The side of her face was buried in his chest, just below his collarbone. Sublime God, giver of life and good fortune! You, Ahmed Ibn-Mustafa Al-Bahairi, I thought to myself, have wasted your life! I ran outside the house to find a shady tree to sit under while I collected myself and poured out what was in my heart. I felt that I loved Simone with all my heart and that I'd never loved anyone before her, and that Zeinab may have married me, but she had never loved me. I felt I'd wrapped my hands around an empty space, that there was nothing more than a mere illusion between them. And I found my sorrow too great to be dispelled through my tears. Finally, I fell to consoling myself by thinking maybe Hamid and Simone were going through the same thing as Zeinab and I. After all, who really knows what hearts hide and walls conceal?

THE DIARY OF
MAHMOUD IBN
AL-MUNSI

Friday, August 10

Today, Hamid Al-Bahairi travelled by himself in his red car to Cairo to close a deal for the importation of some products needed for his business in Paris — Arabic foods in particular for his hotels and restaurants — and to see some of his Egyptian friends whom he had met back in the City of Lights. His trip was to last five days, after which he would return to prepare for his departure from Darawish next Friday.

But before Hamid said goodbye to Simone and rode off in his car, he entrusted his wife to his brother Ahmed's care. Then he charged me to make sure she passed five enjoyable days and filled my pockets with all

I might need to cover the expenses of Simone's wanderings in Darawish and the surrounding area. Frankly, I was happy to bear these responsibilities. I was to plan out her days, hour by hour, as I did for myself with my daily schedule of diary entries at home. Hamid added that his brother could accompany us in our walks if he wanted to and had enough time.

Then Simone hugged him and kissed him standing beside the car on the agricultural highway, and Hamid got in his car, turned on the engine and drove off as Simone waved to him with a white handkerchief and yelled out her wishes for a pleasant journey.

Meanwhile, Ahmed Al-Bahairi sat appalled by what he was seeing with his own eyes, embarrassed before the men sitting in the coffeehouse who began clapping their hands together and shaking their heads in amazement as they called for God's protection against temptation, apostacy and Death's torment.

Simone wanted us to walk together for a while along the agricultural highway before going back to the house. She tactfully asked that Ahmed was not to and gave assurances that she would return quickly. I relayed all her wishes to him, until he understand what she wanted, said goodbye politely, and walked back over the bridge.

Simone told me that she was happy about Hamid's trip since his absence would free her from those formal visits and allow her to really get to know the people of Darawish and the true character of our village. At the same time, she said, she really would have liked to be with Hamid, exploring Cairo for a few days. But he had promised her yesterday to extend their stay an extra week after leaving Darawish to visit Cairo, Luxor, Faiyyum and Alexandria. She also told me she was anxious about the problems in communicating with her mother-in-law and Zeinab that would be caused by her limited Arabic vocabularly, not to mention their ignorance of French. For this reason, she told me, I should stay close by at all times, even at their house. I promised her I would and assured her I had nothing else to do and that I would be at her service at all times. She squeezed my hand in a gesture of thanks. I felt so happy that I had come to know Simone.

We turned to go back along the agricultural highway toward Darawish. Simone seemed solemn. Her head was bowed slightly and her attention seemed to be elsewhere. I thought she was feeling that she was suddenly alone in the midst of a people totally alien to her, and I think I even saw her wipe away a tear that had welled up, in spite of herself, with the corner of the white handkerchief that she had used to wave goodbye to Hamid. But she quickly raised her head once again as she neared the Al-Bahairi house. She surprised me a little when she said to me that she planned to shut herself in the house until the following morning with Zeinab and Hamid's mother in order to rest and also to get to know her mother-in-law and sister-in-law better. Then she laughed and shook my hand to leave me until the following morning. After she went inside, I became self-conscious, suddenly noticing the eyes all around watching me, which I hadn't been aware of while with Simone, and I picked up my step as I hurried back to my house.

It is unfortunate that I didn't begin writing these

memoirs on a daily basis from the time Simone and Hamid arrived, but the idea only occurred to me as we were saying goodbye to Hamid. I cursed myself for not having thought of it before. From the start I should have been recording Simone's presence in Darawish, or at least as much as I knew from what I'd seen and heard. But to tell the truth, I'd been overwhelmed by their frenzied activities which never seemed to slacken. I was amazed to the point of shock by Simone's vitality as she attempted to comprehend Hamid's adventurous life in Darawish and across the seven seas. So now, I would like to go back and mention what happened during the past week.

Simone and Hamid had attended a number of banquets, meetings and official visits since arriving. These functions took place either in Ahmed Al-Bahairi's house or in the house of some prominent figure or the Maamur and once in the house of the District Manager himself. The invitation was always for lunch, dinner or tea and I was inevitably part of it, staying alongside Hamid and Simone to help those present with French words and phrases or with English, in which Simone was also proficient.

But the strangest of these visits was one we paid to the museum and house of Ibn Luqman in Mansura. Simone had requested this visit herself, and the Maamur had arranged it for her the following day, last Wednesday. She wanted to see the prison where the French king, Louis IX (Saint Louis), was once held captive. She saw the room and the shackles. Then we went to the garden of 'Shagarat ad-Durr', and we told her a story about what Shagarat ad-Durr did when her husband, the king, died.

On our way back to the car, while we were still in the garden, Simone leaned toward me and said: 'Tell me, did the jailer, Sabih, really castrate the king?'

I answered her with honesty and open embarrassment over her question, which betrayed the extremes of her people's beliefs about us:

'Really, I don't know.'

She persisted saying, 'What does the word '*Tawashy*' mean then?'

I said, 'I don't know that either, but I'll ask.'

She continued: 'Fine. What is its French equivalent?'

I shook my head at her, expressing my inability to answer, but quite unable to say the word 'eunuch' to her. Promising to have the answer for her soon, I cursed that poet who had once written a famous verse that had made it all the way to Paris:

'The chains endure
And so does the Eunuch Sabih'

I wanted to talk to her about the 17,000 who had died at the hands of her people in this battle and about those who'd died in Darawish and about the pregnant women whose bellies had been split open in order to determine whether they were carrying males or females. I wanted to talk about the way they impaled live ducks and chickens over slow fires with long sticks pushed through their bottoms until they came out their mouths or necks; and about the villages completely destroyed and razed to the ground by Napoleon's Army. But I took into account her position as my guest and remembered that she had no part in what happened and had not shown the slightest malice or sarcasm in her tone or expression when she asked her questions. But who knows whether or not this European face might be able to hide behind itself things the eyes can't see and the ears can't hear? But then again why deal with her on the basis of a presumption, since presumption is a punishable sin?

Last Tuesday at the Maamur's house over glasses of unholy drink, Hamid opened up to us all more than I had ever seen him do before. He told us the story of his life. He had escaped from Darawish by foot, walking until he could stow away on top of a railway carriage.

As a boy he'd worked at various tasks, each for a few days only, and usually in a new town, until finally he ended up in Alexandria. There he had the opportunity to work washing dishes on a steamer, travelling everywhere, visiting various ports. His wanderings ended with a job as a servant in an Algerian coffeehouse in Paris. I noted how everyone enjoyed his story.

Yesterday, I went to sit with them in front of the nice cabin on the beach. Hamid and Simone had stretched out next to one another; Hamid raised up on his elbows while Simone rested her head on his shoulder and tried to imagine how a distant French city with a unseen beach might compare with that place. Then she gazed at Hamid, content and enraptured, and quite unworried about his background. The sea was rough, and black warning flags were raised all along the beach. That excited Hamid who gently moved Simone's head off his shoulder, jumped up, stripped and threw himself into the sea. He then began slapping at the waves with his arms as Simone called out: 'Oh . . . Hamid!'

I wanted to stop him or call the lifeguard to come and help, but she took hold of me before I could move and said, 'Don't worry about him. He's just like that. He's really an excellent swimmer. . . He swims like a fish.'

The lifeguard came over and blew his whistle and called out a warning. Then he put a life belt around his neck and was on the verge of trying to save him and to bring him back to the beach from the roaring, crashing waves. But just then he saw him coming back. He came over to protest Hamid's conduct, but when Simone gave him a silver riyal he smiled and began praising her husband's swimming ability. He went on to request that she keep him from diving in again since the sea was as treacherous as Death herself and her angel, Azrael. He also mentioned to her that Azrael usually stayed in the sea when he wasn't busy claiming some soul. He added that at times Azrael liked to amuse himself with people who barged into his house when the waves were crashing together to make his bedtime music. Simone laughed a great deal as I translated for her all of these things which he seemed to be making up as he went along, and she gave him another riyal.

Meanwhile, Hamid came over panting and with water dripping from his face and hair. He went into the cabin to shower, and I told Simone that Hamid had suffered and endured a great deal in his life. I said that he and his life story were an example to me. Simone just smiled and said,

'He has experienced life.'

Hamid returned and sat down happily. He ate a few eggs and a piece of romano cheese, and Simone poured him a cup of hot tea from their thermos. He could really have been Parisian, if it had not been for his dark complexion, his thick, wavy hair, his dark eyes and his ears whose tips stuck out from his slicked-back hair as though they were constantly straining to hear something just beyond earshot, not to mention his sunken eyes beneath his heavy eyebrows.

On the other hand, he could just as easily be an Egyptian but for the luster and vigor of his face and the bit of pink in his skin color down to his collar, probably from all the wine he had drunk and all the pork he had eaten, or from the multitude of hot and cold showers he'd taken in recent years and his constant attention to his intake of vitamin-rich fruits and vegetables. I was not without envy for his lively, vigorous body as well as for the emotional strength I sensed in him for Simone and her love for him. I rationalized his superiority to myself by thinking it was a matter of luck, and that this was his lot in life. When he chose risk as his path in life, that path could have easily flung him into the abyss of poverty, illness and despair. But I can't put myself in his place. In what sense is he a son of Darawish? We have all come to be one people and each understands the other, since Hamid came to us and we saw Simone.

Yesterday, after returning with them from the beach, I left them and went back to my house where I found a letter waiting for me from Medical School informing me of my acceptance as a student with a tuition waiver based upon my academic achievement. Today I forgot to mention the news to them (or at least to Simone). Hopefully, I won't forget tomorrow. If my efforts to help them are successful, I'll be changing my plans for the future. For ever since they arrived, I've been dreaming of life in Paris, of studying in Paris, and obtaining the highest degree possible, a medical doctorate, in Paris. They should be able to obtain a study grant for me as a token of their gratitude, if they wished. They could also provide me with support while I was in Paris, for which I would be indebted to them the rest of my life. I would be prepared as well to work for Hamid in Paris, in his hotel or in one of his restaurants in any job that he might assign to me. My knowledge of French and English is passable now and will improve immensely in the coming years. But I must be cautious: I can't ask for all this openly. The important thing is that Simone should be pleased with me and also be fond of me. And if she falls in love with me so much the better, since at that point, she herself might present the idea to me and then talk it over with Hamid. Perhaps she wouldn't even need his help. After all, she is a journalist, and people like her have influence and know their way around. It's just up to me to be careful, kind, intelligent and devoted . . . especially the last three things — kind, intelligent, and devoted — things I don't always feel the need to employ in my dealings with the people of Darawish.

Saturday, August 11

Today was the first day we spent together by ourselves, walking outside Darawish. I wore a fancy shirt and slacks for the occasion, but found Simone worried that I might damage them. She asked me to wear walking pants and dark, short sleeved shirts during the day. Her own very simple look surprised me. She had tied her hair in a bun and wore a short-sleeved cotton blouse and short pants (shorter than the underpants my mother wears) and her camera was slung around her shoulders.

As we left Darawish we were bothered by the usual

stares from rooftops and from behind windows or half opened doors.

Just outside the town Simone saw an ancient sycamore tree standing beside an old water-wheel dating from the days before farmhouses began to spread through the area with each year. She took a picture of the sycamore from several angles, then climbed up on it with glee, but I stayed behind since my clothes weren't appropriate for tree climbing. Then we entered a heavy thicket of reeds and bulrushes until we were overlooking a pungent pool of stagnant water. We walked along its edge guarding carefully against falling in until we'd finally made our way out of that nauseating and repulsive brush. Simone's presence made me sense the meaning of things around me more than I had before — their smells, their colors, their component parts. Some children had relieved themselves at the edge of the thicket and the wind had spread the smell in the midday sun.

As we stepped away from the brush she saw the Nile for the first time, running a short distance from our village. She shouted with surprise and delight and scolded me for not having brought her to see our great river before. She made a comparison between its blueness and its width and the narrow, brownness of the Seine. I told her its water was sweet-tasting as well, then found her suddenly taking the camera off her shoulders and beginning to unbutton her shirt.

'What are you doing?' I asked.

She replied very simply: 'I'm going to swim across the river and then come back.'

I said that she should not do this, and she became

afraid and asked me if I'd said this because there were crocodiles in the river. I told her that the crocodiles were all south of Egypt blocked off by cataracts, locks and dams. Then I explained that the peasants and children of the area suffered from diseases contracted from the river water, and she said that she felt very sorry for them. She took a few pictures of birds, palms, acacia and mulberry trees along the banks, then she took me over to a field where we picked some cucumbers and washed them with water from her thermos, which she had been carrying in her bag in defiance of my offer to carry it for her.

We sat under the shade of a tree near a neighboring village, where all the people working in the fields had already seen Simone in Darawish and knew who she was. Perhaps they had even been waiting for her to come and visit their area since they showed no signs of surprise at seeing her or at seeing me in her company. They came over to meet us and gave us even more cucumbers, then they roasted ears of corn for us, and Simone chatted with them. They all seemed to like her. They also talked about her a great deal in their own tongue, which she couldn't understand. I, of course, didn't bother to translate their expressions of desire for her and regret for the inadequacy of their own women. But they never went beyond mere words. I, myself, tired a great deal during this visit since I was responsible for relaying all that she said and most of what they said. They put her on a donkey bare-back, and she took a picture with the donkey and several pictures with them. The encounter ended with her shaking each of their hands in gratitude and, as we left, she began talking to me about them. She commented that they were a generous people in spite of their poverty and poor health.

Then she asked, 'Why don't you use any machinery on your farms?' In answering her, I referred to our ignorance, overpopulation, lack of capital and British Imperialism. She, again, expressed her sympathy and apologized to me when she saw me become emotional about these subjects, as though she herself were the cause of all that had happened, or as though she'd opened up an old, forgotten wound in my heart.

We came to the hills at the outskirts of the town. Throughout our walk, Simone had looked to me like some tourist trying to discover everything about a world that she had not known previously. She behaved like a child seeing the world for the first time, full of chatter and bouncing with life and happiness.

We ate lunch in town at the Al-Rahwan restaurant: fried fish, fish soup, rice and sauce. The owner himself brought her a cold Aswan beer. She drank some of it with her lunch until she became slightly intoxicated, then she forced me to drink with her. Since this was the first time in my life, I quickly became drunk. I began to lose all my inhibitions and I told her that I loved her, at which she laughed and said without a trace of annoyance:

'Monsieur Mahmoud, you're drunk. Let's go back to Darawish now.'

I became embarrassed with myself and agreed that we should return to Darawish. We went back as far as a coffeehouse on the river overlooking a port with some fishing boats and a large ship ferrying passengers to a summer resort. We sat on a round balcony on an upper floor where we drank more beer, and I became so elevated and light that Simone took the bottle from me and poured it into the river saying, 'I beg your pardon, Monsieur Mahmoud, but you've had enough.'

We left the coffeehouse as the sun angled toward the horizon, and Simone announced her desire to return to Darawish by way of the river. So we rode back a way in a small boat, the best of the ones in the port. I was in no condition for rowing so Simone had to take turns with the boatman, until she tired and lay down on her back at the end of the boat where she rested and contemplated the horizon's seductive roundness. Then she turned over on her stomach, looking over the side of the boat and playing with the water's rushing froth. There in the middle of the river with the waters rushing around us I didn't think to warn her about Bilharzia microbes. I was too content watching her as every fibre in my body stirred, and the breeze played with my hair. But I didn't go beyond mere fantasizing. I contented myself, in that awful silence, with my dreams of her and me.

Simone waved goodbye to me at the Al-Bahairi's door. I was supposed to return two hours later so she could, with my assistance, chat with her in-laws.

When I returned to my house I was only too aware of the problem of the beer smell on my breath. I quickly rinsed out my mouth with bicarbonate of soda, then chewed some mint leaves, then ate dinner. After that I hurried out of the house to take a walk along the agricultural highway so that no one would smell my breath. All the while my head was still floating with rapture.

I went to the Al-Bahairi's house at the appointed time, and Zeinab opened the door for me, saying sarcastically: 'Please come in . . . The "señora" is on fire.'

I went into Simone's room after I'd knocked, and she'd asked me to come in. A record album was spinning on her gramophone and she was sitting near the window with a serious look on her face writing a letter. She asked me to go into town for her tomorrow to have it mailed to Paris. Then she began to show me the pictures in her album as the music played in the background. Our heads were so close together that the scent of her Chanel perfume ran up my nostrils into my head stirring in my breast the passions of adolescence. I tried to pull myself away from her, but I couldn't until the door opened suddenly with no warning and I saw Ahmed Ibn-Mustafa Al-Bahairi standing in the doorway, saying to me: 'How very nice, I must say! Get up and out, Sonny boy.'

Simone asked me what he was saying and I told her.

'He's just letting me know my father wants me.'

'Fine,' she said. 'Go on, and then come back after a while.'

I moved toward the door actually intending to leave, but Ahmed blocked my passage at the doorway, suddenly seizing me and saying, 'Wait a minute. You at least have to translate for us.'

I looked at him and noticed the command in his eyes. Then I turned toward Simone and went back over to her causing her to ask, 'Why aren't you going to your father?'

'Monsieur Ahmed says he doesn't want me 'til later on,' I said, 'after I'm finished here.'

Simone looked at me dubiously, then turned to Ahmed. Finally, she decided to ignore the whole affair and stood up. She told me to tell her brother-in-law that she wanted to eat dinner on the roof in the moonlight.

'At your service, my fair lady,' he answered.

The roof had been flushed with a large amount of phenol and cologne after being cleaned, and the chickens had been shut into their coop. It smelled like a pharmacy during an epidemic. A mat was rolled out and a rug unfolded over it, with pillows placed around the edges. Simone sat beneath the pale yellow moonlight. I was placed on one side of her with Ahmed on the other and her mother-in-law and Zeinab across from us, aping her manner of eating, and smiling at each other in open mockery of their guest. I don't think it was lost on Simone either. All around us, the eyes of our neighbors stared over piles of hay and firewood from the neighboring rooftops, some nearby and others at some distance.

We finished our dinner, and Simone opened a large envelope containing a collection of photographs of her family which she began showing to her mother-in-law, as well as to Zeinab, Ahmed and myself. There were pictures of her with her parents and of her with Hamid, in their house, at school, at the hotel, at the restaurant, on the street, on the Champs-Elysées, near a broad boulevard, in the museums and near the Eiffel Tower. Ahmed paused a long time looking at the pictures of the hotel and restaurant, while Zeinab paused over the Parisian women in the background of the pictures. The mother-in-law, for her part, took long hard looks at pictures of her grandson and granddaughter, and even went so far as to praise their beauty and grace. Simone gave her a picture with Hamid and both children in it. She was delighted by her mother-in-law's great joy at having the picture and by her request that Ahmed frame it and hang it in the living room to celebrate her grandchildren. I thought I smelled something rotten about this as I observed Ahmed and Zeinab's agitation. The envy in their movements and eyes was obvious. I only hoped that Simone, who was, I believed, unfamiliar with this sort of jealousy, had not noticed anything.

Simone changed her position, her thighs tightly pressed together and her legs crossed and folded under her to one side, when suddenly she jumped and turned to me saying accusingly: 'Monsieur Mahmoud, did you tickle my foot?'

I was startled for a moment; then looked over at Ahmed who was sitting on the other side of her next to her legs. Then I said with innocence: 'No, I didn't do it.'

She then turned to Ahmed and said to me as she stared at him, 'Tell him I am faithful to my husband.'

I looked first at Ahmed, then at Zeinab, then back to Simone before saying, 'I can't.'

'Why?' she asked.

'His wife will know,' I answered.

'You're so sensitive, Mahmoud,' she told me.

Then she shocked me by turning to Ahmed Al-Bahairi and using an Arabic word I'd never heard her say before.

(She'd probably heard Hamid saying it occasionally to his children.) Without changing her seated position she said to him in Arabic: 'Naughty! Naughty!'

Zeinab picked up on the exchange and stood up, trembling and staring down at her husband. She wanted to speak, but her words all crashed into each other in her mouth before she could say anything and in the end she ran off. Ahmed's embarrassment showed as he stood and excused himself to go to sleep. Once he'd disappeared Simone laughed and said to me, 'All the better. Now maybe she'll stop running after Hamid, and he'll stop flirting with me.'

The mother-in-law, being hard of hearing, was unaware of anything that had happened. We all got up to descend from the roof, and I said 'goodbye' and left to go back home.

Monday, August 13

I was unable to write in my diary yesterday. I was far too busy. Simone went out with me into the streets of the village and we entered several homes. We had long conversations with the men, women and children of the village. But I was not guiding her. Instead, she was moving me through my own village. It occurred to me that she must be taking all these pictures and talking to all those people because she intended to write about Darawish and its people for the Parisian paper she was working for.

We went to the coffeehouse where she drank a luke-warm bottle of lemon-and-lime soda and told me that she did, in fact, intend to write a number of articles about Darawish. She also informed me that a woman had come to her yesterday before we met and asked her about a treatment for her daughter's sore eyes. On the spot she had pulled a bottle of eyedrops from her purse, a couple of drops of which she had squirted into the little girl's eyes. She added, 'That little girl's head was filthy. I took her to the bathroom and rinsed her head with water, then washed it with shampoo.' She became excited as she went on, 'Can you imagine, Monsieur Mahmoud? There were lots of tiny insects in her hair!'

I was overcome with embarrassment for Darawish and I said, 'Her family must be very poor.'

Simone shouted in protest: 'What are you saying, Monsieur Mahmoud? You have plenty of water here. What about your Nile, Monsieur Mahmoud?'

When I went back home, my mother talked to me about what a disappointment I was becoming, wasting all my time with 'that French woman.' My father added that she was corrupting me, so I walked out in anger and went to sit in the coffeehouse until the Omda sent for me just after sunset and I went over to his house.

I found Simone there sitting with him and his wife and the other wives of the village leaders. Of course, I had to be present amongst all these women to serve as translator. The evening lasted until after midnight and was filled with food, talk, tea and songs sad enough to rend one's heart. Nafeesa, the village beautician, danced directly in front of Simone. She sang her a cheerful song, then a song for work and an elegy, for one who's been killed. Simone particularly enjoyed the elegy so I translated its lyrics for her as she copied them down, and I tried to use a moving language that would make it into something a little more special — but, to be honest, it was like trying to get blood from a turnip.

Later in the evening, long after midnight, the Omda and I escorted her back to the Al-Bahairi house. Along the way, I asked her if she wanted to go tomorrow (that is today) to the summer house. She said she couldn't go tomorrow but would like to take me up on the idea when Hamid was along. She said she planned to lock herself in her room tomorrow since she had so much to do, and she wanted to get on with it. She had to write letters and make notes. She wanted to record some observations and asked me not to come except for lunch with Ahmed, Zeinab and her mother-in-law. When we'd arrived at the Al-Bahairi house, Zeinab opened the door for us. When Simone went inside, Zeinab turned back to us and said, 'Good night, Mr. Omda.' Then she slammed the door in our faces leaving the Omda to curse her and her husband all along our return route until we parted.

Today, I left my house an hour before my appointment at the Al-Bahairi's, so I could stop by the coffeehouse and sit there until lunchtime. When I went over to the Al-Bahairi house I found a large group of women and children standing in front of it and pushing through its entrance into its living room. When I looked in to see what was happening, I found Simone inside putting eyedrops in the children's eyes one after the other.

She saw me and cried, 'Monsieur Mahmoud! Come, help. I've worn myself out all morning and haven't been able to write a thing.'

I came in to help her, amazed by her zeal and asking myself how she could possibly have brought so many of these little bottles lined up beside her. Ahmed then informed me, as he sat laughing sarcastically at her predicament, that she had asked him to go to the town that morning and buy the medicine after all these 'little bastards' came to her.

As lunchtime approached we completed the ministration of the eyedrops. Ahmed chased away the little parasites and shut the door behind them. Zeinab began setting out the pots of food — most of it boiled as usual — and Ahmed knocked on Simone's door to call her to eat.

Because Simone had not been able to get into her work and had failed to start her writing that morning, she excused herself from our evening program, and I left her until the appointed time the following morning.

THE SIEGE

Um Ahmed

It started on Monday morning. Some of my old friends, all getting on in years, came to visit: Um Khalil, Um Ibrahim, the Hajj Tafeeda, Lady Nazeera, and Saniya Hanim. Some had had children and money, others had seen neither husband nor children, only living out lonely lives. We were sitting huddled together in the open area on the roof under a bit of shade in the heat and humidity, all because of the Lady Simone, the Frenchwoman; we were trying not to upset or bother her. We'd left her in peace and quiet.

My friends had wanted to see my foreign daughter-in-law again and sit and chat some more with her. But the orders of my son, Hamid, and Ahmed after him, were clear that we weren't to go near her. We were to leave her be, and she would sit with us or go out or shut herself in her room as she liked.

The Hajj Tafeeda beat her breast and bellowed, 'My darling sister, since when does a woman tell men what she wants to do?'

Then Saniya Hanim said, 'But, my sister, this is a French woman . . . a foreign Madame. The whole town and all its people are at her beck and call.'

Then Lady Nazeera said, 'But how could it be? The name of the Prophet protect and preserve him, isn't Hamid one of us? How could he leave her like that to do what she pleases?'

Then Um Khalil said, 'She pokes around with her hair all undone in the fields and back alleys. And always with that boy, Ibn Al-Munsi. Why they even saw her drinking beer in town!'

Then Saniya Hanim told her, 'Like her husband Hamid, but then again she was raised that way.'

Now Um Ibrahim spoke, asking me: 'And the Lady Simone — God bless her heart — what might she be doing now?'

I told her, 'She's writing to her family in France. They say she's also writing about Darawish for her country's papers.'

This had all my friends sucking at their lips, and Um Khalil said, 'We've lived it all and seen it all. But in the end, we'll all be dragged through the mud in her papers.'

Then Saniya Hanim said, 'God pity us. We haven't been to school and we have never once worked for ourselves. We are all of us living as though we were the living dead, whether rich or poor.'

Then Lady Nazeera said, 'Health and life, and in the end, may God grant us a "happy end."'

Then Um Khalil, that two-faced viper, asked about my daughter-in-law Simone, 'Is she a Christian like the other foreigners or did she convert to Islam and become one of us?'

I told her what Ahmed had told me, that she'd kept her own family's religion; then she came right back and asked me slyly,

'And the boy and the girl, will they be Moslems like Hamid or Christians like their French mother?'

Then my other daughter-in-law, Zeinab, making her own private judgment, said with a smile:

'The boy will be a Moslem like his father, and the girl a Christian like her mother.'

We all laughed when she said this, but Zeinab claimed that my son Hamid had made this agreement with his wife, Simone. But I challenged her over this, saying, 'How could his own daughter, from our own flesh and blood, be a Christian?'

At that point Um Khalil said, 'You none of you know your heads from a hole in the ground. You're making guesses without really knowing a thing. Whoever told him in the first place to leave all our chaste Moslem girls and marry a Christian and a foreigner?'

I felt like my blood would boil over with anger, at Hamid, and at Um Khalil, and I asked Lady Nazeera, whose husband taught in the Mosque, what Islamic law said about mixed marriage, 'Isn't a Moslem man permitted to marry a Christian woman?'

Then this wise woman answered: 'God is all-knowing, my sister. That's correct. Islamic Law permits the Moslem man to marry a Christian woman.'

Then Um Khalil said, 'Sure, I know. Give her your verdict, you and your husband. You're always ready to permit what's proscribed and proscribe what's permitted.'

Then Lady Nazeera added, 'But God also says, "The Moslem girl is preferable for a Moslem." I heard the Sheikh say so with my own ears . . . just a few days ago.'

Finally, Lady Nazeera made us change the subject by saying, 'By the Prophet's life, we've been talking enough.'

The meeting on the roof went on and on. Then my friends all left because the Lady Simone hadn't stepped out of her room since morning. If they'd only waited a little while, they could have seen her like a hospital nurse treating the eyes of the village children, talking and giving orders, as my son Ahmed listened to her and obeyed.

I went to watch her and, shocked at her aggressive conduct, asked myself, 'Has my son Hamid married a man?'

Zeinab, all the while, was swearing and cursing — Simone not realizing she was the one being cursed — because now Zeinab would have to clean the house again and sweep up the footprints of the women and children, all for Simone's sake and while Simone, herself, was locked away in her room. Ahmed sat there the whole time like a dumb animal, scared to say so much as a word to stop her and keep our house from becoming a free clinic.

In the afternoon, Lady Simone went into her room and closed the door behind her. Lady Nafeesa came to me then to sit with me on the roof and began whispering in my ear things which shocked and angered me.

She said, 'Simone, the wife of your son, Hamid, doesn't shave the body hair under her armpits or between her thighs.'

I knew she was partly right. I'd seen her armpits with my own eyes when she ate with us. But I told her I couldn't believe she didn't remove that other hair as all our women do, either with hot ashes, red earth, or hot putty made from molasses or melted sugar with lemon.

Then Lady Nafeesa told me: 'The proof is in the pudding. It's up to us to examine.'

'What do you mean?' I asked her.

She didn't answer me. She just went on, saying:

'Simone, the wife of your son, Hamid, who could have used his youth and money to buy any of a thousand women just like her, is not circumcised like other women — or even young girls in our village for that matter.'

'How do you know?' I asked.

She waved her hands around and said, 'That's the way things are in her country.'

Suddenly, I felt half crazed and angry. I said to her, 'If that's the way things are there, and Hamid is happy with the way things are, let him do what he likes.'

Then she leaned toward my ear to say, 'Listen to me, Auntie. If one of our women is not circumcised as a girl, she is on fire, like a cat in heat. She demands men and is never satisfied. She wears her man out every night and she cheats on him at every chance. Simone must have done it so many times, both before and after getting married.'

Then she added, 'Look for yourself. Don't you see your son, Ahmed, running after her . . . he and Mahmoud Ibn Al-Munsi? She laughs at all the men. She walks into every house, sits in the coffeehouse with the men and drinks the wine that corrupts even the men themselves if they should fall into its trap.'

I didn't want to believe her. I began assuring her that my daughter-in-law must have been circumcised as a child, or at least after she married Hamid. My son, Hamid, would never agree to leave his wife in such a state, throwing herself at any man. Nafeesa just laughed and went back to saying:

'The proof is in the pudding.'

'How?' I asked.

'We'll give her a check-up,' she said. 'No one will know. See no evil, hear no evil.'

But I was afraid and told her, 'But if my son, Hamid, finds out. What then?'

'He'll never know. Simone is a woman like us and will be too embarrassed to tell him what we've done to her. Also we'll keep her calm by telling her why we did it.'

Nafeesa's words drifted into my ears and convinced me. I made an appointment with her in the evening when Ahmed would be praying at the Mosque before he went to the coffeehouse to spend the evening with the men of the village. I told her to bring Um Khalil and Um Ibrahim but not to talk to anyone else. I was to convince

Zeinab. I was sure she would agree to help because I knew that she was jealous of Simone and would be happy to see her humbled.

Zeinab

The whole affair looked to me like a game of blind-man's bluff. I told myself that surely even if Hamid found out what we'd done to Simone, he wouldn't be able to do anything about it. He would get a little angry, then resign himself and forget the whole thing. But still, he'd know then that his wife is no better than I am, and certainly no cleaner. He'd realize the Egyptian woman is better than the French woman a thousand times over. And Ahmed would also know that I'm better than Simone with her light flesh and delicate bones, and that he should accept a woman like myself with open arms, poor and ignorant as he is compared to his brother Hamid.

Even if Hamid and Simone did leave us in anger . . . To hell with them and their money! I'd rather relax and be rid of the torture of her company, and his, and of constantly having to grovel under their feet like a servant. Then Ahmed would come back to me, humbled before them, and be there at my own feet every night.

Ahmed had gone to the Mosque for the evening prayer. We had all gathered on the roof of the house: my mother-in-law, Lady Nafeesa, Um Khalil, Um Ibrahim and myself.

The French woman was still in her room listening to her music box and writing and dancing. (I'd watched her many times through the keyhole). I'd also checked up on her about an hour ago by bringing her tea in her room. She was writing away like some sort of lawyer. I hated her with all my heart and envied her whole world. Her luck on this earth had been so much better than mine. Her husband was better than mine, and one picture of her two children was better than all my five children in the flesh. Now finally, the time had come to satisfy my lust for revenge and chill the raging fire in my heart.

We came down from the roof without a sound. I led the other women to her room and opened the door. She was dancing.

She jumped when she saw us. Maybe it was something about the look in my face that scared her, or maybe the sight of all the women behind me. I said to her (knowing

101

that she couldn't understand what I was saying), 'You have visitors.'

Then I pushed the door all the way open to let the others in. She jabbered a bit in her native tongue, greeting us (or perhaps damning us, who really knows?), and Nafeesa laughed back at her. Then she sighed in surrender and turned off the music with a push of her finger. She started to collect the papers spread out on her table. Then she spun around suddenly when she heard the sound of Um Khalil slamming the door shut.

There was no way for us to talk to her. Nafeesa closed the window and we surrounded her. She reeled around terrified, looking for a way out. We grabbed her. The screaming was frightening us, so I covered her mouth with my hand. Then we threw her down on the rug in the middle of the room, and we raised the ends of the ample skirt she was wearing. She wasn't wearing anything under it. We were holding her tightly, and she was fighting with all her strength trying to free herself from the four pairs of hands.

Then Nafeesa said, 'Didn't I tell you?'

With those words she began cleaning Simone up first with her scissors, then with hot putty made from molasses, clearing away all that filthy hair between Simone's legs.

Then Nafeesa snorted and said to my mother-in-law, 'Look, didn't I tell you? She's not circumcised!'

Nafeesa was still working with the putty while Simone's body trembled between our hands, when Nafeesa suddenly proposed that we circumcise her, there and then. The women were all enthusiastic about the idea, and my mother called out, 'Why not? What's preventing us? . . . but what if she tries to make a scandal out of it?'

'Don't worry,' Nafeesa said with confidence, 'She won't make a sound.'

She had finished up the shaving business and now pulled a small bottle of anesthetic out of her bosom. She took off its cover, and the smell of chloroform wafted out. Then she took out a piece of cotton, also hidden in her cleavage, soaked it in liquid from the bottle and put it over Simone's nose.

In the light of the lamp I saw Simone's eyes open as wide as they could, filled with horror. For a second I thought I would save her: push all the others away from her and help her up. I was imagining myself in her place. But then I thought of how intoxicated Hamid must be by her wild spirit—not to mention her body which was as white and soft as Turkish delight—all because she was uncircumcised.

Her body went limp beneath our hands and she stopped fighting. The suppressed moans rising from her lips stopped, and her eyes shut for a second, then stayed half-open, and I told myself, 'It's started now, and it must be finished. We shouldn't stop here. What's been done has been done, and we've got to finish it. Even if we did stop now, Hamid would be no less angry.' And I assured myself he'd cover the whole thing up to avoid dragging his wife and himself into a scandal.

Meanwhile, Nafeesa began doing her work with obvious delight as the others stood around, relaxed, and watching her sacred and sublime operation with extreme excitement and satisfaction. She pulled the thing out as far as she could with her hand, then used her other hand to take out of her pocket a sharp straight-edged razor, like the ones used in shaving. She opened it out, wiped it on her clothes, then pressed down and flicked its sharp edge quickly until the flap of flesh came off, she held it between her fingers, and a river of blood burst forth. None of us had seen so much blood in all the ceremonies we'd seen performed on village boys and girls.

Nafeesa started to press down on the wound all the cotton she had to stop the hemorrhaging, but the pieces of cloth kept soaking up the flow from that hapless woman. Nafeesa used both her shawl and Simone's shirt, pressing them into the wound for a long time. But the blood kept coming. And the cloth was soaked in a sea of red.

My mother-in-law slapped her cheeks with her hands and cried out, 'What a disaster.'

Nafeesa's face went pale, then the faces of the other women blanched as well. Our shocked and horrified voices mixed together while Simone lay, motionless, totally unaware of what we'd done to her or what we were doing now. Nafeesa screamed at us to shut up lest we bring a scandal down on our heads and demanded that I bring her all the coffee grounds, ashes, and red earth I could find, and I ran out stumbling and falling all over everthing as my knees trembled beneath me.

I brought Nafeesa what she'd asked for, and she began scooping up handfuls and putting them on the wound: first the coffee, then the ashes, then the red earth. Then we waited. First the coffee grounds were soaked, then the ashes, then the soil. The bleeding colored it all red, then stopped. I wanted to lift her up on the bed, but Nafeesa ordered me to leave her as she was until the wound had dried.

Then I saw a sight I'll never forget. It was my mother-in-law. Something long asleep in her suddenly woke up. She picked up the razor and turned toward Nafeesa. The women all ran out of the room and escaped into the streets. Nafeesa, meanwhile, began backing away from my mother-in-law muttering, 'I didn't do a thing, I didn't see a thing.'

When her back touched the door she felt for the door knob without turning around. When she finally found it, she fled out of the house and escaped.

Um Khalil, who'd stayed behind, said to my mother-in-law, 'Patience, Um Ahmed. She won't be hurt badly. It's God's will, we are all slaves of our own destiny.'

Then my mother-in-law turned toward her and she too fled the house. Then it was just my mother-in-law, Simone and myself. My mother-in-law opened the window, spat on the razor, and flung it into the fields; then she closed the window again and turned to me. She pulled me by my hair and shook me, but I didn't fight back. In fact, I wanted her to kill me. But she let go and turned around and began slapping her cheeks again. She squatted down beside Simone and put her head in her lap.

She bent down and kissed her forehead and whispered to her passionately, 'My darling! My daughter!'

Then she began to rock back and forth and cry, 'You came here of your own free will, from your own land . . . To be tortured.'

She looked at me in fury and said, 'And you! Why are you standing there like that? Why didn't you stop me? I've grown old and crazy. But you . . . you're still young, and healthy in spirit . . . Healthy? Hah! . . . you were jealous of her, you and Nafeesa, and Um Khalil. All of you! All of you! I want to cry . . . but I can't. I want to cry just one tear, but it won't come. Oh, scandal of scandals! My little girl! Hamid! My darling! Oh, scandal!'

She was still rocking back and forth while she talked, and the sight of her and the words she was saying tore my heart to pieces.

She paused for a moment then screamed in my face, 'Hurry up! Go break an onion. Bring me some cologne. Wake her up, Zeinab.'

I ran out and broke an onion and came back with a bottle of cologne which Simone had given me as a present along with a handbag and some dresses. We held the cologne under her nose, then poured it out all over her face. I tried massaging her chest and squeezed the onion under her nostrils, then Simone began sluggishly moving her head in the lap of my mother-in-law, who called out to her: 'Simone, my darling.'

Simone groaned and blinked her eyes a little. She cried up to me weakly as I stood over her, then managed a wan, fleeting glance before her head lolled to one side, her eyes still half open.

'She's dead,' I screamed. 'Mother! She's dead!'

A roaring sound surged out of my chest. My mother-in-law began cursing me, not wanting to believe she'd died. She tugged at her arm, realized that she was dead and began slapping her cheeks again. Slapping. Slapping. Slapping . . . as she rocked back and forth with the head of Simone still resting in her lap.

The Maamur

I had to deal with the situation promptly, what a scandal! If the Omda had been in my presence at that instant instead of having telephoned me at home with the news, I would have shot him dead on the spot. How could such a thing have happened to the sweet and gentle Simone? And in my region! What is this barbarism that I must rule over and live in? Even toward foreigners! . . . and toward women! . . . *Bird from the East? The Saint's Lamp?* Ha! How could we have fallen so low? I pity you, Hamid. The Siren called to you, and you came over land and sea to lose your most cherished possession, here in your own homeland.

I gave the doctor a ride in my car and informed him of everything that had happened, just as the Omda had relayed it to me. Then I left him alone a while to think about how he would act. I considered the idea of arresting the Omda, the village elders, the night watchman and Ahmed, and whipping them all mercilessly until they died. But if I did that, I told myself, I'd simply be repeating the same thing Darawish's damned women, those hags in black, had done.

I asked myself, what is it that makes us envious of beauty and leads us to want to crush it with our bare hands? Like the lamps, whose light changed our nights into day. And Simone . . . poor Simone.

I consoled myself with the thought that what had happened to Hamid and his wife had been carried out by his mother and sister-in-law, and right under the nose of his inattentive jackass of a brother. But was there any consolation for Hamid in what had happened? Of his own will he walked into his eternal torture. If he'd never left his country none of this would ever have happened. If he'd never left Paris, responding to the call of the Siren, none of this would have happened. If . . . if . . . if . . . I think I am losing my mind.

'What will you do?' I asked the doctor.

He answered without turning to face me, 'Maybe she's still alive.'

'And if she isn't?' I said.

'Then she will be dead,' he replied, like an imbecile.

I asked again, 'What will you do? How will you handle it?'

He threw me a cold stare without speaking. I said:

'And what about us? The cause of death. Listen to me. Whatever the cause, it need not become public knowledge or ever leave the confines of this region.'

'How could that be?' he asked.

'Fix it,' I said. 'You're the doctor. You must know a thousand causes of death.'

I was thinking to myself that life itself could be reason enough for death. Then he said to me, 'What about justice?'

I answered firmly, 'Look, I'm not a judge. Think of the scandal. Think of my destiny and the destiny of every official in the district. And your destiny, and the position of the government in all this.'

'And if I did it,' the doctor said. 'Who would protect me against informants going to the authorities?'

'Listen,' I said. 'If there are any informants they'll never get to the authorities, even if they go through the mail.'

He said, 'And Hamid? Who would protect me against him?'

'Leave him in God's hands for now,' I said helplessly. 'For now, the important thing is that you order her immediate burial.'

Then he went back to 'And Hamid?'

'We'll send for him as soon as we've finished everything,' I said.

We entered Darawish and the doctor and I got out of the car followed by the assistant officer and a soldier. We left our cars behind us at the bridge. It was a dark, black night, the moon having disappeared about an hour ago. I found that all of Darawish knew what had happened and had already started to add to it. There was a large group of them surrounding the house. I issued an order that everyone return to his home, then sent out the soldier and the night watchmen to enforce the order sternly by beating any violators with the utmost severity.

I entered the Al-Bahairi house and found the Omda sitting with his head bowed. I spoke to him harshly, and he stood up before me. Then I raised my hand and slapped his face, and he cried. I saw Ahmed standing against the wall in a state of shock. I felt like seizing his protruding Adam's apple with my teeth and ripping it out of him; but I spat in his face instead. He didn't even raise his hand to wipe it away. The doctor had gone into her room. Something inside me wanted to see her. But I was afraid to confront death— hers in particular. I kept pacing up and down in the living quarter until the doctor came out and closed the door behind him. After a moment spent staring into our faces, he said, 'She's dead.'

And then he wrote out a paper, which he gave to me saying, 'This is the burial permit.'

Then I said in a loud voice for all to hear, whether they were present in the room or not, while I winked at the doctor from the corner of my eye: 'How did she die?'

He answered with an icy coldness, 'She died as a result of a cardiac arrest — severe and sudden.'

Then I repeated his statement in a loud voice, 'Did you all hear? She died of heart failure. Understood?'

Then I told the Omda, 'Bring a carpenter to prepare her coffin. We'll bury her tonight in the family cemetery plot.'

And I turned to Ahmed and said, 'Did you hear that? In the family plot. So you can remember her always. You and your mother, your wife and all of Darawish, you scum!'

Ahmed moved his mouth a little and said in disbelief, 'Coffin? With no washing of the body?'

'Silence,' I screamed in his face.

He went dumb, and I sat trying to think what I should do to Nafeesa. I decided she shouldn't escape punishment, no matter what the official cause of death.

When the living quarter emptied a little, I took the doctor aside. He, the assistant officer, and I were the only ones left in the room. The two of us sat down. I thought briefly about the unbearable ordeal Hamid would be going through tomorrow. It would all start tomorrow and continue whether he stayed in Darawish or fled back to Paris. Then I thought about how Simone had died and that this doctor knew death as well as he knew life. I whispered:

'Tell me. What was the actual cause of death?'

The doctor had been off somewhere in a daydream. Finally, he said in confusion, shock still written all over his face, 'Right, huh . . . whose death are you talking about . . . our death . . . or hers?'